THE SLEEP OF THE RIGHTEOUS

THE SLEEP OF THE RIGHTEOUS

Wolfgang Hilbig

Translated by Isabel Fargo Cole

Two Lines Press

Originally published as: *Der Schlaf der Gerechten* © 2002, S. Fischer Verlag GmbH, Frankfurt am Main

Translation © 2015 by Isabel Fargo Cole

Published by Two Lines Press
582 Market Street, Suite 700, San Francisco, CA 94104
www.twolinespress.com

ISBN 978-1-931883-47-4

Library of Congress Control Number: 2015934426

Design by Ragina Johnson
Cover design by Gabriele Wilson
Cover photo by Gallery Stock

Printed in the United States of America

This project is supported in part by an award from
the National Endowment for the Arts.

ART WORKS.
arts.gov

The translation of this work was supported by a grant from the Goethe-Institut, which is funded by the German Ministry of Foreign Affairs.

GOETHE
INSTITUT

Contents

Introduction

László Krasznahorkai
Translated by Ottilie Mulzet

The world, from the point where Wolfgang Hilbig existed, was bleak and desolate. It is only his sentences—wondrously quotable, visionary—that give color, light, indeed, in a certain sense, even a kind of magnificence to this bleak and desolate world. But how is this possible? How is it possible to create linguistic magnificence from what is for Hilbig a bleak and desolate world?

Many have already written about Wolfgang Hilbig, but this is worth nothing. Because the secret of Hilbig—and there is a secret!—remains undisclosed. Hardly anyone knows about him; he remains largely unknown in translation, and even in Germany—despite the fact that he should have received every significant literary prize—he is practically unknown. Here "practically unknown" means that the literary public doesn't know about him, the critics don't pay any attention to him, and if it wasn't for the publication of his works by the highly influential publisher S. Fischer Verlag in Frankfurt, and moreover, had there not been, in Hilbig's lifetime, a few—really just a few—older critics who mentioned his name with appreciation (although no one pays attention to

1

them anymore either), then in all likelihood, at least in the short term, he would completely disappear from our view.

Many have thought and have said about him that because his fate and writerly art are so closely tied with Communist East Germany, Hilbig is just little more than a kind of chronicler of East Germany, a pale Kafkaist—and the Germans themselves don't like this kind very much. Hilbig's art, to wit, and with no further prevarications, is built upon the fact that East Germany is identical to the world. To put it more precisely: for Hilbig, East Germany is the world, because what is beyond it does not exist for Hilbig; it could not even exist for Hilbig; for beyond that hideous juxtaposition that was the East German response, within the Soviet bloc, to the Soviet bloc, that is, beyond that particular individual version of the Soviet type of pseudo-Communist dictatorship, nothing, for Hilbig, existed. For him nothing existed; there was no world beyond this! For can there be yet another world beyond the world? he would have asked uncomprehendingly.

Moreover, no German identifies, especially not willingly, with this point of departure, with this frightening identification. The western, northwestern, and southern Germans— that is, the free Germans, the Germans who built West Germany during the Cold War—generally like to regard the East German Soviet-type dictatorship as a purely political formation, the horrific everyday existence of which they love, even today, to hear and read about voyeuristically: a series of everyday occurrences with all its secrets and disclosures, which was valid exclusively for that East German Germany; which, with its own everyday life, collapsed, disappeared, came to an end. Whoever reads Hilbig quickly understands that nothing ever ends, and there is especially no end for the Germans, because those ordinary days contain within themselves a force: base, frighteningly motionless, dark, lurking in the depths, a monster that has not collapsed, that did not disappear; even today it lurks there in the depths, frightening, threatening, dark, just as if it were always there. People never ask themselves: why did Kleist do away with himself? And in general: why do the Kleists keep doing away with themselves in such a world? No matter how unexpected and perhaps even unfounded a leap of judgment it may appear to be, Hilbig lived those very ordinary events that were part of the everyday lives of Kleist or Büchner or Lenz.

The horrendous, deathly, unquiet, baleful, murderous everyday situations of the petty bourgeois. These routine occurrences do not pass. The petty bourgeois does not pass. A world comes into being through these everyday events, and these are the mundane situations that Hilbig lived through during the decades of the East German pseudo-Communist dictatorship. He did not write about the particular East German pseudo-Communist dictatorship, but about German everyday experiences.

More precisely: about everyday life.

And this is what is so oppressive in Hilbig. With horrific strength, with evocative sorcery, with obsessive precision, he described a world that is distasteful not only to Germans but actually harrowing for all of us who sense the unbroken strength of those ordinary events. He wrote his astounding novels about a world in which only the weak, the sensitive, those incapable of bargaining and in no way heroic, can sense the chaos and the surrealism. Because this world really does have its own rules, and there are those who realize and maintain its organizational structures, since this is their world, a world in which the aggressive, mean-spirited, cowardly, servile—namely the rat-person, running away from the monumental, the far-reaching, escaping from freedom—is the lord, pursuing at his pleasure those who are alien in his world, which he creates again and again; the alien, those who don't belong there, whose existence cannot be legitimated—indeed, the unfortunates who cannot legitimize themselves.

Wolfgang Hilbig is an artist of immense stature. He discovered a wondrous language to describe a horrific world. I admit this is a sick illumination. Nonetheless, it is illumination. Unforgettable.

THE PLACE OF STORMS

1

We could claim but a small part of the street: our street, as we called it, stretched townward to the point where the pavement began—uneven and jolting, made of square granite cobbles—and out the other way to the railroad crossing, where the town, at least its inhabited part, really had already ended. The sedate, brassy clanging when the red and white gates were cranked down—a sour note made by a tiny hammer striking the inside wall of a shallow, bowl-like mold—was, in a way, the town's death knell, for past the railroad crossing, at least on the right side, lay vast fields of rubble with looming black beams and ruined walls: the remains of munitions factories where concentration camp inmates had labored in wartime.

Our part of the street had not been paved yet, except for the narrow sidewalks outside the two rows of apartment blocks. Between the sidewalks was but a straight track of sand, perhaps once light, now since times unknown black-gray, as though in proof that a mix of many colors ultimately yields darkness. Coal dust and ash had blackened it to the pith, and then had come the reddish mass of crushed brick, the rubble from bombed-out houses that was used to even the surface. After each rain you gazed into a bed of murky, viscous mud; in the dry spells of summer the street was an endless reservoir of dust that advanced all the way into the stairwells and seemed to glow in the midday sun; it covered barefoot boys' skin up to the thighs with the black bloom of inviolability.

We little kids, bored in the long days of summer, sat on the curb, our feet in the dust of the gutter, puffing on cigarettes, their smoke barely visible in the sun's glare between the façades. And we sat on the steps outside front doors that were always shut against the dust; from a distance we seemed a visibly degenerate mob unlikely to lift its siege of the sidewalk without a fight. Passers-by crossed the street when they saw us, or turned onto a side street beforehand, seeking the shelter of the large trees, the chestnuts or the lindens; our street lacked trees and saw hardly a shadow.

At that time there was a dearth of men in town; most of the children were fatherless, and many remained so forever. Time refused to pass, bearing down on them like a weight that stunted their growth. And the sole liberation from boredom lay in growth, in the adulthood that all the others had achieved some incalculable time ago and no longer wasted a word on. And the books we read, the stories we made up and told, as a rule featured only adults, and for the most part only men. — The mere thought that you were still *small* made you sick, you sickened with boredom ... There were no fathers to take pride in your growing up after them. Or they were mayors, policemen, pharmacists, teachers . . . or miners, waiting for their pensions, so tired in the evenings that they never spoke a word. — For the mothers, it seemed, you always stayed a child, they seemed to forget you had a name, all your life you were *the child* for them, eternally neuter . . . and I heard my mother calling me, in the rooms, in the hallway, across the yard, through all the floors her clear voice rang . . . Child, she called, where are you? Where've you been all this time? — And when we crossed the railroad tracks to reach the strip mines, or entered the woods that began beyond the expanse of ruins, when we vanished all day from our street, out of reach of the town and adults, in the evening she cried: Just look what the child's been up to again, just look at the child, what a sight! — She cried these words even though I'd returned intact, almost entirely unscathed, giving no cause for concern whatsoever . . .

It was an affront: for a time whose end seemed out of sight you were condemned to the life of little kids for whom the months, the years passed only in arid theory, in the form of a convention the adults were set upon; any actual passage of time would occur only in the intangible future. It was a stuffy, stubbornly opaque doom that hung over the whole town, but over our street with special vividness: there were no fathers there to make still littler children.

Little kids was our collective name, rarely heard without a touch of scorn, which seemed to vanish only when the big kids on our street wanted something from us. They'd say, for instance, "here, have a smoke"; we ignored the condescension, put on finicky expressions, and helped ourselves. Pensively we'd roll the cigarette between thumb and forefingers until someone offered us a light. We'd have loved to strike a match on our boot heel, something we'd never seen done. But we'd eavesdropped on grown-ups who'd seen it in movies in the American zone of Berlin, for us an utterly unreachable continent. We'd never been to the movies, not even to one of the town's two movie theaters; besides, we lacked the boots for the purpose. The big kids struck matches on the glass of shop windows; we'd seen that and tried it ourselves when we could get our hands on a matchbox—in kindergarten and later at school the possession of matches was seen almost as an act of sabotage—but our matches wouldn't light, or rarely lit, on the glass panes, and usually the indignant shopkeepers chased us off.

Once we'd lit the cigarettes, the big kids came out with what they wanted: it would seem to be some risky matter. When they had a ticklish task for us, they avoided the word *kid*. But since such jobs required someone who looked particularly harmless, an indirect disparagement remained. — Apparently I never really looked harmless, and so the jobs regularly went to those who were even smaller, or a half to a full year younger than me, with my eccentric birth date. — We'd offhandedly promise to look into the matter; in reality we rarely did a thing, and had to spend a while on the run from the big kids. But they swiftly forgot what they'd needed, or it would prove superfluous; after a time we sat on the curb once again, bored and unmolested, awaiting our maturity.

And this waiting was contradictory: on the one hand our goal was to grow older, to rise at last from the state of useless, unfinished, in-between beings; on the other hand, perhaps still worse than the alternative, that would thwart any permanent alliance with the power of the summer in our street. — For we saw how the adults suffered from the heat; we nodded understandingly, even chimed in with their laments, we cursed along with them when a yearned-for storm refused to come and the thunder bogged down above the woods in the east. In reality, though, we took in the incandescent air as though every trickle of sentimentality had to be parched from our innards. We breathed the smoke that rose from the furrows and faults in the street dust, we took in the afternoons' paralyzing stillness like the golden-yellow vapors of alchemistic smelters, which made us younger, yet lent our faces the ancient grins of African demon masks. — If it ever did rain at night or in the morning, the midday sun leeched all the moisture from the furrows of the road, from that one lane of deep ruts that led across the railroad tracks and all the way out to the strip mines . . . and after a thunderstorm had indeed come, when the sky was white-blue again, the ruts were transformed into two channels of water that reached to the calves, and on the surface floated a fine film of reddish ash.

In winter the street was frozen rock-solid, with the menacing glitter of frost in the petrified mud's recesses. Every day now, with torturous slowness, the cumbersome ash carts passed, so broad that on our stretch of the street there was room for just one at a time. They were welded together from strong, rusty steel plate, and the remnants of paint not yet burned away were rust-red as well. With bodies that tapered toward the bottom to ease the dumping of the ash, they resembled armored battleships; swaying slightly, grinding and groaning, they crept out of town in a cloud of exhaust;

the fat, black, rubber tires clearly found little traction in the sometimes iced-over ruts of the street. The ash carts left a lingering wave of salty fumes between the buildings; you tasted it, felt its sting in your throat and your lungs, and long after the carts had passed the air seemed roiled by invisible, burnt-smelling waves. The trapezoidal monsters hauled the fuel waste from all the households and the rebuilt industrial plants out of town and dumped it in the first of the mine pits...the first mine pit had once been the largest, though only the deepest half contained water; in the meantime it had been filled by ash, rubble, and rubbish to become the smallest of the so-called "final voids." — The wagons were drawn by prodigious brewery horses, just as rust-red as the ash carts, steaming and grinding away just like them. High on a wooden bench sat a driver swathed in black and dusted with brown ash, clicking his tongue constantly and puffing on a charred, crooked pipe. With their shoes slipping on the frozen mud crests, now and then the utterly phlegmatic beasts would stop; the coachman's long, arcing whip, tip flicked out, sank from the white sky onto the horses' huge rumps, darting there artfully until the mighty animals, making reluctant fluttery sounds with their nostrils, resumed their trot once more; fine wisps of ash rose from their coats as the man on the wooden seat administered those tiny, well-aimed rapier jabs that sometimes cracked like distant gunshots.

One day, two of the poor beasts had fallen into the ash just as the wagon was unloading, and dragged the entire vehicle along with them. — We were told this by the railroad gateman; he hardly spoke a word otherwise, but the accident had horrified him too deeply to pass over it in silence. The pit's crumbling rim—only the frost, he said, had lent it a deceptive stability—had given way beneath the weight of the wagon and team; the driver was standing alongside, and only a quick-witted backward leap saved his life. But the horses, snarled in their harnesses' tangle, slid with the wagon down the steep slope to the bottom of the mine, where they sank into the subterranean embers covered only by thin layers of cooled ash. The beasts' bellowing whinnies . . . no, their shrieks, said the signalman, must have been heard all the way to town; the whole area was filled by the rank smell of burned hair and flesh. — My grandfather, said to love horses more than people, had come running to the ash pit from his nearby allotment garden, clutching a shotgun, but before he could reach the site of the accident the horses had already fallen silent; death had seized them. All the same, the men shot from above to make the heaps of flesh stop twitching, but it was no use. And in the end, the weeping driver hurled his tobacco pipe down into the depths of the mine pit!

Much later, I recalled reading of a similar scene in a long book I'd never finished: a captain by the name of Ahab had likewise flung his pipe, his last remaining pleasure, over the bulwarks into the ocean's rolling waves, disconsolate at his failure to chase down a huge white whale he'd been hunting for nameless ages across the seas.

In any case, the accident spelled immediate ruin for the horses' owner, Bodling the carter, a friend of my grandfather's. It seems he then took to delivering beer, driving the beer and soda crates to the shops and picking up the empties with a rickety little three-wheeler. As the town's other carter was unable to cope with all the ash by himself, the town government eventually drummed up a new motorized garbage truck, but it took the rest of the winter and nearly all the next year. In the meantime, people carted their ash out of town themselves in wheelbarrows; after dark they emptied the bins right into the ruins beyond the railroad crossing... to the gateman's chagrin, but he said nothing, he kept his silence. And when things got really bad, people began to fill the ruts in the middle of our stretch of street with ash, which transformed it altogether into a hilly, barely negotiable waste, in the spring thaws emitting a medley of noisome smells that burned off and vanished only in summer.

My grandfather's gun had become a kind of legend in town, at least in the part of town within our ken and control. It suddenly made me an object of interest for the bigger boys on the street who had consciously experienced the war. For them the war had been decidedly more exciting than the peace, the post-war period that increasingly metamorphosed into a regimented existence full of inevitable demands that could not be escaped, with time gradually divided into fixed units that had to be faced, the main thing being punctuality and reliability. Peace, this much seemed clear, was governed by the clocks, time by the clock had taken power, and quite quickly one realized there was no more escape from the power of the ordered time blocks. It was no coincidence that everyone told how the Russian soldiers who had chased away the war and brought the peace—it seemed, unfortunately, that they'd chased war away for good—were especially keen on the watches the vanquished Germans wore. When the Americans were still in town, no one had cared about German watches, nor had the Americans cared about time and order. They had left that to the Russians who replaced them soon after the peace began—and you could tell from the Americans' grinning faces, it was said, how little credit they gave the Russians with regard to order and time management. They were mistaken; the Russians installed town administrators who were downright obsessed with cleaning up. Cleaning up and rebuilding…order and cleanliness; these, one sensed, were especially tenacious German virtues, and the Russians were well aware of it. But the Germans—at least some of them, even adults—weren't so keen to play along, and went on dumping their ash and their rubbish in the ruts of our street by night; only those, of course, who didn't live on our street themselves. Thus, peace meant for a time that the street was fouled by the acrid smell of sodden ash, mingled with the vapors from rotten vegetable scraps and fallen, liquescing fruit; unprecedented populations of bluebottles and wasps appeared out of nowhere to take over the street; and more and more run-over rats were left lying in the space between the sidewalks and had to be disposed of. The scourge ended only when policemen began to patrol the street by twos in dark blue uniforms, one member of each pair armed with a revolver.

The rubbish disappeared, but the police patrols remained, pacing the street not just by night; soon they were seen in the daytime as well, and if the bluebottles and the vinegar stink of the trash hadn't already driven us from the street, the gaze of those policemen did. They eyed us suspiciously, and it was impossible to smoke in front of them. We decamped past the city limits to the strip mines, suddenly finding ourselves in the big kids' midst, though we were far from belonging there.

This incurred the disapproval of my mother, who regarded the whole area past the railroad crossing as one great danger zone.

Child, she said to me, you're not big enough to go to the strip mines by yourself. You don't know your way around there, and you can't swim yet! — By the way, she never neglected to mention, when I was your age I'd been swimming for ages. — Go to the swimming pool instead, she said. I'd know you're in good hands there. — And she gave me the twenty pfennigs to pay the cashier. There was a wading pool for small children where no one could possibly sink; I was decidedly not a small child anymore, but you were inevitably shooed away by a pool attendant if you came anywhere near the big pool with its diving platform.

I saved up the admission fees for other purposes: by day I was out of reach for my mother, who worked in the cooperative store at the other end of our street, and along with the others, as unsupervised as I, I kept on going to the strip mines. — There we found ourselves amid the groups of big kids, where girls and boys already mingled, and all at once talk turned back to my grandfather's gun. They approached us—we were lying, still dressed, in a grassy area apart from the noisy bathers—and I noticed, not without gratification, that I was the chief focus of their attention... my mother wouldn't have liked that either.

Suddenly they'd lend me their dog-eared books—this had sometimes happened before, one being the story of Ahab the one-legged whale hunter, missing a good many pages, which was why, apart from the book's heft, I quickly lost interest in it; those thin, cheap paperbacks printed in double columns, all from West Berlin, were much more enthralling.

They generally related the adventures . . . or rather the cease-less shoot-outs of a recurring, invincible character whose name was emblazoned on the lurid covers: *Buffalo Bill* or *Tom Brack the Border Rider* or *Coyote, Rider of the Black Mask* . . . I devoured the books by the kilo, and I needed to read quickly, as they always had to be returned a day or two later or passed on to someone else who was desperately awaiting them. My mother watched with extreme disapproval, believing this reading material would forever corrupt me to the core. — Suddenly the big kids bestowed their cigarettes on me alone and left the others out . . . after all, I was the oldest of the little kids, and, I sensed, was gradually growing to catch up with the big kids.

But all they cared about, more and more disappointingly, was the mysterious gun, which Grandfather refused to let me see. — When we hunkered in the grass cross-legged like Indians, the shadows of the bigger boys would loom behind us—at once I felt the suspicious gazes of the adults, a few of whom always mingled with the beach crowd—and, darken-ing the sun, they leaned over and whispered: Is it a carbine? A hunting rifle, double or single? Or is it a small-caliber gun? We'd have the ammunition for it . . .

At the center of attention, I would have loved to say: it's a Winchester! — That was the kind of rifle the pulp novels were always talking about.

Some time when we came, couldn't we bring the gun along . . . ? Only then we'd have to go over to the marsh to bathe, where we wouldn't be disturbed. Or we'd have to fix a meeting place in the forest and bring the gun there!

I never thought of denying the gun's existence; I had

doubted it myself until I heard the gateman's story, but it brought me incredible prestige. However, I could think of no good excuse for its remaining beyond my reach. So I half agreed and half refused... This constant talk about the gun would attract way too much attention, I said.

Do you think we'd rat on you? they asked indignantly.

Not that, but it's awfully risky if too many people know about it, I replied. And day by day I went on stalling; on the one hand the big kids got on my nerves with their constant interrogations, on the other hand I feared losing their attention; that would have meant foregoing the bounty of new pulp novels, whose contents floated in my head, nearly monopolizing my thoughts. Should the supply of books break off, I knew, I would have to make up stories like that myself...

The mine pit beaches were not always peaceful places: the big kids took great pleasure in mounting so-called mud fights... and not just them, also the female contingent of the beach crowd, who retreated into the background, cheering and applauding from a safe distance—depending on which group of combatants they'd sided with—when a shot hit home with a smack. — Using your hands, or shovel-like objects, you'd dig up fat, sticky chunks of clay and loam at the edge of the water and shape fist-sized balls you'd pile up around you, and once each group had sought out a spot with enough cover, behind hillocks, behind the reeds, or behind the low, leaning trees that sometimes loomed in the reeds... spots close to the water, so new balls of clay could be fetched as quickly as possible... when all were at their posts, battle was joined with a great roar. When the foe broke cover and ventured an attack, the command came: "Barrage!" and a volley of projectiles flew through the air until the attackers had retreated again—only strategically, of course, for the attack had drastically decimated the other side's supply of mud balls. Someone charged with bringing a fresh supply of clay would have to break cover, coming under a bombardment that would nearly fell him if he failed to seek shelter in deep water... and maneuvers like these were celebrated twice as loudly. The whole thing could go on for hours, and ended as a rule with one of the parties capitulating, usually by announcing they'd run out of ammunition. They were ordered to come out with their hands up, and when they did the last of the balls were fired at them, though only up to their thighs; anything else would have been dastardly. — Given the nasty consequences when someone was struck in the face by one of the smartly thrown, heavy, compact clay balls—especially when the ball had previously been rolled in loose gravel to compound its effect—what, I asked myself, would happen if one of the fronts... and sometimes there were three fronts, of which the third, weakest one regularly confederated with the one that had the best prospects of victory... if one such front had suddenly had my grandfather's gun on hand...

I need bathing trunks, I said to my mother one day; at the swimming pool you can't go into the water without bathing trunks. — It was a lie, if only because I virtually never went to the swimming pool. — I used to go there myself as a child, mother said, and as I recall, children always got to use the wading pool without bathing suits. But all right, I'll knit you some bathing trunks.

And mother knitted me bathing trunks of a size... some day I'd go on growing, after all... that was generously assessed. She had just enough elastic band for the legs, so the trunks were held up by suspenders knitted from the same dark-blue yarn. They were attached with large buttons; on my back they formed the letter X, and in front, on my chest, they described a broad H. I knew at once that I couldn't go to the big mine pit in these bathing trunks; who knew what epithet these suspenders would have earned me. Perhaps the name *Hix*, which sounded like the rickets or the hiccups... or like that one-legged hopping game played by very small girls amid an enigmatic configuration of squares drawn on the ground with a stick or with chalk; I could picture nothing duller than that game. So I went back to the marsh, to the ever-shrinking mine pit where I had first gone bathing. It was the pit closest to town; a hole just a few hundred yards across had remained, and as more and more ash was dumped into it, one day it would vanish utterly, a melancholy thought.

The bottom of the strip mine, as well as a flat dry expanse on the other side, past what was known, with great exaggeration, as its "beach," consisted of a layer of peat-like lignite that had not been worth mining. This layer had quickly been ignited by the glowing cinders; across its full breadth the coal seam was being eaten away by the blaze and gradually turned to ash. From the edge of the pit you could see how far the blaze had advanced: along an irregular line the nearly black ground was displaced by the pale gray, nearly white fields of ash that crawled further and further forward. Bit by bit the ground was pulverized... but beneath the thin crust of cooled ash, broad swaths of embers glowed on; neither beginning nor end of this deep-reaching hellfire could be explored without risk to life and limb. Nothing could extinguish the fire, creeping inexorably toward the water; I pictured how one day, not long from now, the strip mine's shallow water would explode into a filthy white cloud of steam. Slender tongues of water were already asimmer; even now the little lake was so anomalously warm that one might suppose it was being heated from below. And when thundershowers poured down into the hollow, the entire surroundings were filled at once by towering fountains of steam that in certain winds fogged my grandfather's glasses in his allotment garden and made him shut himself up in his summerhouse until the fog, which rendered the garden's narrow paths invisible, had passed, dripping as a burnt-smelling dew from the leaves of the fruit trees. — Even on sunny days the atmosphere above and around the mine pit seemed seized by a feverish unrest, distorting every image that caught the eye. The air above the whole terrain had a bluish tinge, and it was as though each glance toward the other side had to penetrate an irregular wall of glass behind which everything was warped, doubled, and refracted. The woods that began on the hills beyond were shrouded and seemed set in constant motion, a ghost forest flickering without end and wavering to and fro, and from the edge of the small lake that was the pit's lower depth, blue tongues of water shot across the narrow beach and up into the forest undergrowth, which looked like a layer of gray-blue rot in which all life was stifled, leaving nothing but hectic spectral unreality. Blue lightning bombarded the gravel face of a broken-off escarpment, wearing it further and further down and making it burrow ever deeper beneath the roots of the woods. And amid the mirages created by the nearly invisible smoke, at their lowest depths, lay the little lake, its water dark brown like coal, nearly black when seen from above, and the blinding abstractions of reflected sunlight flared over its motionless surface: from a distance it was like a puddle of viscous syrup, gleaming golden in the center.

Unreality and semblance held sway over all the area. And I knew that I, as the passage of time willed it, would soon have to grow up...so it was willed by the watches, which—the stories never ceased—were valued so highly by the Russian occupying power, because power needed watches to control the fate of the land...but I knew that even then I'd be unable, long unable, to believe in reality's truths.

No, when I woke in the morning in the far-too-large bed, in the bed that had once been my father's—also a relatively unreal figure for me: in the entire flat there was one single photo of my father, a brownish portrait photo in which he wore a steel helmet...and, as they put it, he hadn't come back from the war, a war of which I knew almost nothing... he had, it seemed, preferred the war to the unreality of the peace I lived in—when I opened my eyes in the morning, I immediately recognized, in the play of dapples and shadows on the ceiling, the simulated character of the time in which I lived, this mere composite of chimerical perceptions... assuming I really did live in this time. I recognized myself in the large dressing mirror on the far side of the room: I saw that I was not my father, that I barely resembled him... though people were constantly claiming I did...I had nothing to do with my father; I saw that I lay in the wrong bed. And yet I believed I could just as well be living in an utterly different time . . . like my unreal father, lingering on in an unreal war, a war vanished forever from a world lost in the wasteland of a half-baked peace. My father, I believed, had given himself or been forced to give himself to an utterly different world, the world of the ice fields outside the city of Stalingrad, and from there he had not returned . . . perhaps one day I could enter this world, if I wrote about it, if I made notes, written expositions which summoned the image of that time into reality once more, as though in this way the present time might become more real. — For the moment, however, I balked at reading my father's letters from the front, of which there were entire stacks: they were written in a strange, spiky old German script that I read with great difficulty; inevitably I would have to have my mother translate the letters. That would be embarrassing; my mother might start crying. Father had such affectionate words for me in his letters, treating me like some quite tender, fragile creature, which was the last thing I wanted to be. At least he called me by my name . . .

But perhaps I could describe quite different times: times in which a solitary rider galloped across the prairie's endless swells, the broad-brimmed hat on his head as black as the horse beneath his saddle. He thunders up a hill, spying from the ridge a group of men instantly recognizable as bandits . . . he reaches for the gun that hangs in a leather holster on his saddle. Without drawing their Colts, the desperados wheel their horses around and flee pell-mell. A slight, barely noticeable smile appears beneath the man's thin black moustache. He knows that the ruffians have only feigned their flight; once out of sight, they'll return to lure him into an ambush. The man smiles; he'll never fall for their tricks . . .

Mother, no doubt, would have called such a story impossible, untrue, and utterly unrealistic. But weren't these made-up stories just as true as ones invented from so-called reality?

There was the story of my grandfather's gun, for instance: it no longer existed, I had known that for some time; I'd heard it once again from the lips of the gateman, and he was credible, if only because he rarely said a word. But in the older boys' minds the gun was still there; they wouldn't stop asking me about it. — The untenable bathing trunks my mother had knitted . . . the most untenable of all conceivable bathing trunks forced me to swim in the so-called *marsh*, the smallest of the mine pits, where the ash heaps encroached upon the water. The water was only a few hundred yards wide, and you could walk from one side to the other; at the deepest spot it barely reached the shoulders . . . you could hardly learn to swim in this puddle. Besides, the brown water smelled so unmistakably of coal, a smell, which clung on late into the evening, that Mother realized at once I'd been to the strip mines, where I wasn't supposed to go. — Why do I give you money for the swimming pool, she said, when you're just going to the mine pits, and when you can't even swim, at that. If only you'd at least learn first at the swimming pool, they've got life preservers there . . .

This caused problems for me, as my friends were also quite reluctant to follow me to the marsh . . . when you came out of the marsh water, your bathing trunks were lined with a layer of wet coal residue that collected there like coffee grounds; one day, when I discovered a drowned insect in these grounds, I got rid of the bathing trunks my mother had made and claimed they'd been stolen. — Stolen! Bathing trunks like those? Even Mother could hardly stifle a laugh at this excuse. Why didn't you just say you didn't want to wear them? — I had chosen an opportune moment; my aunt from Jena was visiting, my mother's older sister who worked as an attendant at a Jena swimming pool. — I can't believe you'd unleash a boy on humanity in such a ridiculous bathing suit, my aunt said. — But the suspenders would've been good for pulling him out of the water—he still can't swim! — If he's going to learn to swim, he needs proper bathing trunks, said my aunt, an authority in the field.

She went back home, and a few days later a small package arrived from Jena containing three pairs of bathing trunks that fit me perfectly: unclaimed items from the lost and found at my aunt's swimming pool. — I picked out a navy-blue pair with a miniature white anchor appliqued to the left side . . . and with them I could return to the largest of the mine pits, between the marsh and another smaller pit. — One day, caught in the crossfire between two warring bands, I retreated into the water and suddenly fell into a gaping hole, for the bottom fell away in treacherous, unpredictable tiers, depending on how the ground had been excavated: I found myself with my head under water, my feet couldn't reach bottom; flailing my arms, I struggled to the surface; with my head back above water I saw the lake's wide, calm expanse before me, one hundred, two hundred yards; the beach lay behind. Instead of yelling for help, I began to paddle my arms—much as dogs do to move through the water—and I paddled, I swam, a sorry sight perhaps, but the water bore me up; I moved slowly, then more quickly, toward the middle of the lake... once I turned around and saw them watching me from the shore, silent and intent... now I had no choice, I had to reach the far shore. I felt more and more confident in my dog paddle, and soon I tried, as I'd seen the big kids do, to swing my arms from my hips up over my head, plunge them in again in front of me, and scoop the water down along my body with my palms, attempting my first crawl strokes... I managed, but it tired me, and soon I fell back into my dog paddle. A few yards from shore I felt a sense of exhilaration; from now on no one, not my mother nor anyone else, could claim I couldn't swim.

When I reached the other side and crawled onto the bank, exhausted, but with an expression as though nothing special had happened, I saw little Will in front of me, stretched out on a plaid blanket in the grass; next to him, almost leaning on his shoulder, sat a female in a bathing suit, one of her hands on little Will's stomach; she removed it as soon as she saw me. Little Will was the brother of big Will, and they were the biggest, strongest boys on our street, both equally big and strong, only the little one was a good year younger than the bigger; both were redheads, and regarded as invincible. It was rare to see them apart, and when they weren't at loggerheads themselves, they put everyone else to flight. Just one by himself was intimidating, and when they made common cause there was no one, even an adult, who could stop them.

So what's the story with the old man's gun, little Will asked me, where is it, when are you finally going to bring it? — I'll bring it, I said, I'll bring it as soon as I can. — On my way back to the beach, circling the mine pit on foot, I knew I'd stumbled into a trap that could have dire consequences for me.

2

In the gateman's lodge we were safe. The gateman, or one of them, the silent, one-armed man, always let us in when he had the day shift. Sometimes, when we got caught in a thunderstorm on the way to the mine pits, he practically urged us to come inside.

You needn't be afraid of the Wills, he said to us, I've got them over a barrel. I know they go out at night stealing coal from the coal trains, I could report them any time I like. Can you picture the hell that'll break loose when the Russian officers find out they're getting coal stolen from their trains? Off to Siberia, they'll say, off to Vorkuta, they've got coal there too!

As Grandfather sat in front of his summerhouse one afternoon with his gun across his knees, motionless, pipe in his mouth, staring ahead with the corners of his mouth turned down resolutely—he was waiting for a marten that had been threatening the chickens in their shed by the house . . . and the chickens were huddled together in a dense mass in the corner, their anxious behavior showing that the marten still lurked somewhere in the tangle of the garden—the police came and took him away. They confiscated the gun . . . it was just an ordinary air rifle, a so-called break barrel, but all the same a pre-war model with considerable punch; grandfather cast the pellets for it himself. He was reprimanded for "possessing an illegal firearm"... an air rifle! — In the evening, after his release, he sat in the kitchen with the same devil-may-care expression... as though still waiting for the marten... unresponsive, he expelled huge clouds of smoke from his spark-spitting pipe. His ancient Polish hatred of the "Russians," easily awoken—he often told us how he'd known Russian occupation troops as a child in southeast Poland—had erupted once again; what had happened to him, he never tired of repeating, was possible only in a "Russki-run state." — Occupying a foreign country always spelled the next war! Stalin himself had said that, he added...

One afternoon I was turned back on my way out to the mine pits: the road was blocked. A crowd of people had gathered outside the house where the Will brothers lived, but, as I saw at once, they kept a respectful distance from what was taking place. The two brothers stood in the blazing heat with their faces to the wall, behind them a Russian soldier with a machine gun, pacing up and down; another, evidently a sergeant, sat on a chair smoking cigarette after cigarette. On an empty chair on the sidewalk I saw two glittering objects: clock detonators, as the gateman later told me, time fuses for explosives; the two Wills had stolen them, no one knew quite where, and half the street was feverishly hunting for a third clock detonator whose hiding place the Wills had not clearly specified. The Russians were drinking, water or maybe vodka, while the Wills got not a drop to drink; hours later the third detonator cropped up, and the crowd dispersed.

That evening I sat alone on the curb, the town transformed in my eyes into one gigantic explosive device. What quantities of munitions might still lie in the ruins past the railroad crossing, in the bombed-out factories where they'd once been produced...and couldn't they blow up at any moment in this heat? — The summer brooded red above the roofs; in the east, where the mine pits lay, it was already growing dark, too soon, it seemed to me. The air that wafted from there through the street bore the leaden smell of smoking ash and smoldering rags. The heat was trapped between the houses, and the vapors seemed to cook. Inaudible tension built up at the street corners; from the side street I thought I heard the crackle of the chestnuts' big leaves drying. Thunderclouds massed over the woods beyond the mine pits, and soon the first lightning lit the sky, followed a moment later by a ricocheting rumble, splitting into intervals of thunder, like mighty metal vats being tossed down from the heights. — But the storms over there, I knew from experience, would never reach the town; they passed the town by when they came from the east...and I believed I knew it was the women who suffered most when the rain failed to pass over town.

Mother forbade me to swim in a thunderstorm, saying that the water attracted the lightning; she was afraid even to go near the kitchen faucet in a storm. — But I had no desire to go to the strip mines by myself anyway; all my friends had been summoned to the police station and aggressively interrogated: Did they know who on our street possessed found ordnance, and where it was hidden?... Strangely enough, I had been left alone. And now they were home, listening to their parents' accusations, and wouldn't be let outside for several days. — Shortly after the incident with the clock detonators the two Wills vanished from town. But they hadn't been sent to Siberia; the gateman told me they'd defected to West Berlin.

As every year, a week before the summer break ended Mother bought me five or six new exercise books, ten pfennigs apiece, which I'd need when school started. This time, though, I filled the notebooks before the start of the new school year, my fifth. Now I was faced with the problem of buying new notebooks myself, which I could only do if I pocketed small amounts of the change I got when sent on errands, or I would have to drum up deposit bottles to redeem at the grocery on the corner; or I could often find a few coins beneath the layer of tobacco crumbs in my grandfather's jacket pockets. The last week before school began was routinely the dullest week of the whole year; I was all alone on the street, my friends busy, kept home by the obligation to prepare themselves for school; the water of the marsh had nearly dried up, only the beaches of the large mine pit were still bustling. I hung about in the gateman's lodge and had him tell me stories; strictly speaking he was the most taciturn person in town, but in my presence he turned talkative. — He let me crank down the gates when a train approached, I just had to make sure the crank wasn't wrenched from my hands . . . I went outside and sounded the death knell that severed our street from the outside world. After that, as the prodigiously long coal trains passed, drawn by two locomotives yet moving no faster than a crawl, I sat at his table again, drinking grain coffee and listening to his voice, soft and hesitant as though he needed a long time to mull each sentence. He was a slim man missing his left arm; the empty sleeve was tucked into the pocket of his uniform

jacket as neatly as though ironed to his body. He had lost his
arm in the war to an exploding grenade, he said, and mark
his words, he'd cheated death by a hair's breadth. And those
sorts, he pointed at the ruins past the railroad crossing, that
lot that kept rummaging in the cellars for munitions and
the like, they'd meet the same fate one day if he didn't report
them all. — What do you suppose it's like out there? he said,
though I hadn't asked. Steppe, nothing but steppe, a hundred
miles of steppe before you set eyes on a house or a village, out
there in Russia. And all dried up in the heat. And then they
set the steppe on fire, and the wind drives the flames toward
you, you don't know which way to run . . .

For me, the Russian steppe merged with the prairie I'd
read of, and the heat that hung over them was more or less
the same. — And forests, I'm telling you, forests . . . blunder
into one, and you'll never find your way out again. No com-
parison with that little copse back there! And he pointed
across the strip mines, where the thunder of stagnant storms
went on and on. — Everything will wither up on us if we
don't get a storm soon . . .

Alone in the flat in the afternoons, I tried to write about
what I'd heard . . . all I managed were images with a prodigious heat looming over them. The flicker and blaze, each new
daily circuit of fire through a terrain I'd dreamed up, this was
almost my only subject, and I couldn't find my way out of it. —
Writing resembled swimming in this sense: once you'd gotten your head above water, once you'd started to swim, it was
impossible to stop until at last you felt the sand of the far
shore. In similar fashion you swam off with your words, born
up by the blood-warm written words as over the surface of a

mine pit smelling of coal and rot... only that there seemed to be no far shore for these words, with the words you had to swim on and on, until the words ended by themselves, until the words themselves went under. But swimming in the words was safe, you couldn't drown in them, you could start over with them the next day... each afternoon, alone while the heat loomed on the street outside, while the heat on the street burned off each last little shadow, when the narrow sidewalks turned hot as stove plates for bare feet.

Men, I thought, without knowing why, could take the heat, they swam through its thoughts as through the shimmers in the air, while the women had spent half the summer lamenting the absence of storms. They were right; this August, oh, ever since mid-July, all the storms had breathed their death rattles over the woods. But women needed the rain, it seemed, only the rain, torrential showers, cloudbursts could fill them with new life. — When I lay in bed at night, sweating even beneath the single sheet, I saw them pass before me, lamenting and wringing their hands on the streets, whole processions of women with their imploring eyes turned skywards, where not the tiniest little cloud showed in the flawless blue. And only over the woods in the east did the dry thunder resound, refusing to approach the town. Before falling asleep I saw it was suddenly they who dominated the street, women no longer young, growing older and older, in their purple or black petticoats: with sunburned shoulders and upper arms they sat on the stoops and waited... Cigarettes glowed between their fingers, and smoke rose from them, it rose in the heat that abated not even at night. I heard them murmur, sleepless beneath my window, a sleepless singsong, a sound of long-forgotten heathen incantations sent up to the sky, where the full moon hung, turning a deaf ear, white-red and immobile.

On the first of September I had to go back to school; the heavens seemed to have heard the women's prayers, for rain clouds hung over the town. It was all the same to me; until late in afternoon I was forced to listen to my teachers' baffling garrulity: history, chemistry, physics ... in that last subject there was something about the origins of storms: it interested me not in the slightest.

THE BOTTLES IN THE CELLAR

The memories pass through old rooms where the furnishings of several generations touch. Things were never thrown away, nothing was replaced, nothing even seemed to become truly unserviceable from wear. The old contraptions, survivors of two wars, held and held . . . no one generation gained the upper hand, and finally I accepted the fact that I did not belong to them.

But the true calamity was the bottles in the cellar, there were bottles upon bottles . . . entering the unlit cellar unprepared, one stumbled just inside the door upon a mound thrown up like a pyramid, seeming, surprisingly, to be formed of earth or mud. Yet when brushed accidentally, thick layers of dust sank to the ground, and an eerily dull dark-green glitter met the eye: the pyramid was a pile of empty wine bottles stacked with the greatest of care, reaching almost as high as one's head, covered over the years by thick coats of coal and potato dust that blackened cobwebs kept from sliding off. And suddenly still more bottles loomed in the semidarkness of the cellar; suddenly, when one dared to look, there were many more bottles still, still more of these pyramids had been started, but foundered, they had collapsed upon themselves, dark green glass had poured out beneath the shelves, it seemed the shelves themselves, crammed full of bottles, had been washed up by glassy waves to freeze, unstable and askew, upon a glassy gelid flood that had rushed shrilly singing to fill every corner. Tables and chairs in the cellar, bristling with bottles, seemed to drift weightless in breakers that in an inexplicable moment had turned into a glassy inlet consisting down to the bottom of shapely yet stillborn and completely soiled bottles: the bottles were empty, it was as though a sea of liquid had in fact evaporated from their necks. But on leaving the cellar one feared one had succumbed to an unreality and would indeed find a sea . . . or, worse still, a sea rolling up insurmountable in the form of full bottles.

Oh, the bottles spilled from the ruptured drawers; if, when seeking an object of deliverance such as a hammer or some other tool, one opened one of the still-shut drawers, one again found bottles, arranged in oddly obscene rows and layers: they lay neck to belly, belly to neck, seeming to copulate in a peculiarly inflexible fashion which was lustful all the same and appeared not to fatigue them in the slightest. And indeed, it seemed as though their permanent unions at once gave rise to the progeny which had slipped behind the tables into the Beyond of now-impassible corners where the bottles had long since entered a state of anarchy and rose in randomly scattered heaps: as if baskets full of bottles had been dumped out, from overhead and at a proper distance, in an attempt to bury the other bottles and finally make them invisible. But the bottles could not be beaten at their own game: there existed ever-new bottles, old bottles, unbreakable bottles of green or brown glass, all of them mute, lapsed into menacing silence beneath the dust of years that swathed and muffled them more effectively than cotton wadding. — The thought of the bottles, of their clearly limitless power, of their unflagging procreation, was the shrillest voice of my sleepless nights. It was not only that I was perpetually waiting for them to pipe up unexpectedly, to cry out in unison . . . my thoughts were so full of their ugly, glassy shrieking that in my head, as in the cellar, there was no room for any other object. I plotted escape, for I lived with an iron verdict: one day I would have to clear them away, one day I would have to free the cellar from them . . . in other words, some day I would have to free myself and all around me from what had become, clear and simple, one main pillar of my existence. It grew unmistakably clear that I, once I had ceased to be a child, would be the only serviceable male in the household: it was a divine verdict, and every day I was relieved to find that I was a child still . . . but time was passing, and in a week, in two weeks, next winter or the following spring it could happen, I would be grown up. I saw that even my threats were losing their effect: the bottles existed on undeterred beneath the grisly symbols on the cellar ceiling, beneath the outlines of the big skulls and crossbones I had drawn on the vaults with the sooty candle flame.

The empty bottles, at least the first of their gigantic assemblages, had been the prerequisites for an ambitious cider production launched in the household at one time. One day my mother brought home what seemed to me a capacious receptacle of brand-new white-gleaming aluminum for juicing fruits, intended to help cope with the garden's yield, which in the late summers began to overfill long rows of huge zinc tubs. That seemed sensible; we were swamped with fruit, even though half the street partook of it. But the garden was stronger: in spring the white- and pink-hued mountains, the sweet-smelling clouds of innocence in which the trees had wrapped themselves as in the aftermath of flowery explosions, showed what we would reap in late summer and fall. Disapprovingly we watched the May thunderstorms, the snow that beset us as late as early June, every year we cursed and insisted that storms had destroyed the bloom—to my secret relief—but even if rain, storms, and hail did damage a tree or two, these severe weather conditions, as they were ominously known in the agricultural section of the newspaper, seemed to have a positively beneficial effect on the remaining trees. And at harvest time they astonished us with an abundance whose approach each summer ought to have alarmed me in the extreme: it failed to do so only because I was effectively not present in the household, I was permanently absent and ready anyhow to definitively abandon domestic conditions at any moment. — The white aluminum receptacle proved an inadequate weapon: each fall it smothered us all over again in the clouds and fountains of a brew that transformed the kitchen into a simmering steam bath, and after nights we spent dancing around it with scalded fingers, trying vainly to penetrate its workings, it collapsed over and over in a mash of brown applesauce, until at last amidst melted sugar, spuming water, and boiling apple scraps it gave up the ghost and had to be taken to pieces and put back together differently. And even as the glowing, crackling bottles on all the tables and windowsills vibrated until they burst, the next invasion of fruit seemed to surge up the front steps; it had long since become impossible to walk anywhere in the house, in the soap-slick pulp on the floorboards pears and apples rolled to trip the feet, and the fleets of fruit-filled handcarts, tubs, and clothes baskets taking up the yard had grown to vast dimensions. I hatched out wild schemes... at night I dreamed desperately of seas across which I fled beneath the fluttering pirate flag, on and on, to regions that knew neither household appliances nor small-town gardens.... Oh, it was in vain that I stole downstairs, in my nightshirt spattered through by sticky juice, to join forces with the goats and pigs against the hostile power: by opening the gate and loosing them upon the freight of fruit...when I was punished for it, it was not because I had imperiled the harvest, but because I had nearly wiped out the domestic animals with diarrhea. — By day, in the still-blazing sun, the fruits finished ripening in the yard...forgotten conveyances filled with early pears were long since rotting in the remote shadow of the washhouse by the time the middle and late varieties occupied the front of the yard...the pavement turned into a swamp of yellow sweetness, honey and syrup oozed out between the disintegrating wagon slats and sank into the gutters in sluggish streams. The buckets rusted, and the baskets seemed to float in one great pond of glistening molasses that made the yard impassable. The invincible fruit, having made a laughingstock of the juicer and its inventor, suddenly began to flow of its own accord, for its own pleasure the mead of the fruit juices flowed and seemed to set even the containers to melting; the fruit washed the yard with a glaze reflecting gigantic swarms of wasps and flies that alone knew no fear of earthly sweetness and whose hordes did not retreat until the juices had turned to vinegar. When the blue vinegar flood transformed the moonlit yard into a tract of hell, when out of false sweetness was fermented the true sourness in which one could hold back one's tears no longer, in which all human skin began desperately to pucker and to crawl, then suddenly it was as though youth were over and done with. — When mold shading from green to black finally gained the upper hand, we had long since gone under... profound fatigue crouched in our hearts, and we were hard put to keep it from breaking loose; we sat about, and our corroded shoes stuck to the floors as seamlessly as madness stuck to the hypocritical calm of our speech; we were too enfeebled to move a finger, and nothing now could dilute the torpor in our veins. — By this time it was already turning cold, the last juices in the yard gleamed like black ice; soon snow would fall on mold and putrefaction. The garden used this time to recuperate its powers, the garden breathed on in its superiority, its denuded, tangled branches reared into the treacherous glitter of the starry sky... and up above, as if to mock us, on the highest branch at the unreachable top of the tallest of the trees winked one single frozen candy-red apple that had resisted all attempts to pick it.

Some few bottles had been filled, and as there was no one who cared to drink the cider, they had outlasted the years. At the very front they sat enthroned atop the first shelves in the cellar. The juice in them, once viscous and brown, had turned into a solid, white-shimmering substance, into crystal, into a petrified mold that had forced off the rubber caps. The mold rose inches above the bottlenecks: these appendages—like the senseless pride of arrogated masculinity—blackened in the fusty air, made these bottles isolated; unable to prove themselves, they could not take part in the festival of procreation at their feet. And so they led the shadowy existence of deposed tribunes, while below them, in the outskirts of their territory, chaos and revolt fermented: the desperate and demoralizing apostasy of the empty-bellied bottles as yet unsullied by nonalcoholic liquids.

I was appalled at first by the desolate petrifaction of the upper bottles; later it was a complex bond with the existence of the mass below that increasingly perturbed me. In the nights when, aided by the contents of new bottles, I attempted to force myself into a murky doze, the incriminating fact of these bottles' emptiness, which in many ways had come about and become irrevocable through my fault, began to horrify me. I had not filled them, the bottles, I had not yet disposed of them; on the contrary, I had bolstered their superior might with more and more treacherous fringe groups . . . it was I who emptied the full bottles to swell their number, a recurring cause of strife, and to establish an inextricable chain of causation: the emptier the bottles became, the more unfillable, and the more numerous the emptied bottles became, the more new bottles I had to procure to be emptied. The more bottles I emptied, the more intense was my desire to do so . . . in my body there was a curse like the very being of bottles: for a fullness in me did not lead to satiety, but flung open ever greedier maws within. — I knew of several bottles, filled with the contents that most revolted me—liqueurs and cloying red wines—hidden away in my aged mother's bedside cabinet. There, in a nook by the head of her bed, behind a hideously clicking door, they awaited guests who never came. There were extremely demeaning nights in which I crept into my mother's bedroom, crawling on all fours along the edge of her bed, inch by inch, trying to reach the cabinet as noiselessly as possible. I opened it, despite my caution causing a metallic snap at which my mother stopped snoring and seemed to listen; for minutes I waited for the noise of her regular breathing to return, the drops of my sweat falling on the floor sounding to me like detonations... then I took one or two bottles from the bedside cabinet, let the door snap shut, again I waited, lying flat on my belly the whole time, until at last I could crawl out of the room with my booty. The way back seemed barely surmountable: I felt as though I had to crawl over endless heaps of empty bottles that sent up no frightful clinking and jingling only because beneath them was deposited the quagmire of several wagonloads of potatoes rotted to mush, combined with cobwebs and soot, as down in the cellar where there was no more room for the winter provisions. This was the morass through which I seemed to worm in nights like that... Darkness, sweat, and thirst were the foundations of my now-adult existence: and in this belly-crawling life my fists trembled with too-heavy bottles which, from sheer weakness, I could barely transport without noise. However evil and stupefying the contents of the stolen bottles, they had to vanish into the cellar as empty bottles that very same night, and the way downstairs, which I staggered rather than walked, the way down to the plane of the bottles, was an ordeal, tormenting me for a long time afterward until sleep finally felled me. It was a feeble sleep in which all dreams turned my stomach: a hundred times I must have seen myself vomit into the toilet bowl, I saw my herbal-bitter heart, my syrup-filled veins, my candied entrails tumble out until there was nothing left in me but dust-black crystal that had to be dissolved in liquids. Droughts laid waste to my throat, my stomach walls burned like desert sands . . . in my body no desire ever could have been appeased: in reality I never could vomit, and there wasn't a drop of alcohol that didn't have its proper place in me. It was something else I wanted to vomit, something imaginary: perhaps it was an ocean, frozen to glass to the very bottom, perhaps it was an earth, plummeting through the night like an overripe apple. Or I wanted to vomit a sleep that brought me no satisfaction because it always had to end again. The sleep that gave me no rest in the nights when, thirsting, half-asleep, half-awake, I listened to the howling of the bottles in the cellar.

COMING

It's as though all through childhood my ears rang from the cries of the women. For a long time I failed to hear them; only later did they reach me distinctly, rising far away, faint, then louder and louder, as through a warren of alleys down which I gradually approached the one street completely filled by them, as by strident songs, a ghastly composition... In my dreams I approach this disharmony of cries; they swell, and when I'm in their midst, when I hear them from all sides, I awaken with a start; alarmed, I strain my ears into the night, which though utterly still I know holds a cry, inaudible only by chance.

The cries ring out through my memory of the years when I was ten or twelve, when I had given up all hegemonic claims within the family and ceased to respond to the cries of the women. Only then did I guess the exact words they spoke, did I think I understood when they gasped out the seeming non sequitur: The lake! The lake! I'm going to throw myself into the lake!

And often it seemed to sound like: *We're* going to throw ourselves into the lake! — But that couldn't be; the term *we*, in this random lot of people cooped up in a tiny flat and forced into a group, had fallen completely out of use.

All women uttered this threat, at every opportunity that arose, it was the most devastating declaration of a ruptured, ever-unraveling communal life; these were words that could come only from the women, whose numbers in the house were incontestably superior: for one of us there were three, sometimes four of them, counting all who fluttered in and out our doors, and the worst thing that could happen was when they sought to unite their voices in a chorus, though they failed, all screaming over one another. — The lake! they screamed, I'm going to throw myself into the lake! I'll throw myself into the lake right this minute! You had to take it with a grain of salt.

These threats were always preceded by muffled sobs— then you still had time to flee—and in the end the words were underlined by loud weeping, quite unmusical, swelling all the louder the longer one delayed one's disappearance. Grandmother, Mother, all the aunts sashaying about our flat, the presumably divorced sisters-in-law who sought refuge with us, the female friends from the neighborhood, all made abundant use of this weapon, and the cousins too, and at last, or so it seemed, even some of my female acquaintances when they dropped by, which astonished me. They had come solely to lend support to the women of the family, I thought, seeing that I immediately forfeited their sympathy, that they chimed in with the others' woeful wails if I left the room even for a moment... What pained them so was my apathy, which I took almost to the point of invisibility: I hunched speechless in some seat in the flat's periphery, and my contours grew fainter and fainter.

Though the first cause of these cries was Grandfather's smoking and drinking, soon that seemed forgotten, and they focused all their vocal force on me. The occasions were arbitrary: my silence was as good as my speech, I heard the cutting words whenever I lied or stole money, when I brought home bad grades, when it came out that I'd cut school, roaming the rubbish dumps outside town or near the lakes in the woods . . . but most of all when, muddy and matted, I came home an hour before midnight, and when I seemed kindled by filthy secrets, burning all the way to my hair's sticky ends, and all the more when I didn't come at all; everything was cause enough for the threat: The lake . . . I'm going to throw myself into the lake!

Come now . . . am I your darling? Come on, tell me! one of the aunts urged, purring, as she oversaw my bedtime washing ritual. — No, I replied coldly, and immediately sensed the sobs rise in her throat; in a moment it would end in the cries I knew so well. — What's he done this time, the little bugger! my grandmother's voice rang out from the next room. He'll send me into the lake yet, that golden boy of yours! — Those last words were directed at my mother, who defended herself, weeping: No, it's me . . . it's me he's going to send into the lake! I'm going to throw myself in, oh yes I am! Dear God, he's just never there when you need him, and it's not like you're asking too much of him! He just never comes when you tell him. And I'm constantly telling him! He's making me miserable, driving me to despair. Every time I tell him: come . . . come home by six p.m. or, fine, by seven, that's when he doesn't come. No, no, I'll throw myself into the lake yet!

When I lay in bed—secretly reading, under the covers

with a flashlight, pulp novels my mother termed smut that would only incite me to brutality and wickedness—I was really only waiting for the flat to quiet down so that I could sneak outside. Silently I shut the doors behind me, groped down the dark stairwell, and opened the rough wooden door to the yard leading to the street with a duplicate key I'd filed to shape myself and hidden in the crack of my mattress. The key was my true secret, and I hid it with a certain pride, having produced it from directions I'd found in my pulp novels.

But my flight might also be noticed immediately, and through the second-story windows, open to the summer night, the sirens of their screams burst out onto the street, so fiercely that the neighborhood dogs began to bark. — He's off again...like a thief, like a criminal! He gets it from that wretched trash he reads. Oh, he'll be the death of me yet, oh, he never listens to me...one of these days I'm going to throw myself into the lake! — Come, come, we've got to look for him, came the reply; but they never followed me, for Grandfather would intervene, slamming his fist on the table: Quiet! He'll come back sure enough...

But in my mind's eye they searched the entire flat for me, as though I might still be hidden somewhere. They searched the closets, under the beds and in the toilet cubicle....they must have read too many trashy novels themselves. And their stirred-up scolding rang out onto the street, above me, before me, and behind me; I was at the center of a musical piece in which all instruments were aimed at me. But I didn't hear it; I'd developed a form of deafness, a mystery even to myself, which I rarely neglected to make use of. When I switched it off now and then to verify that the world still existed, I heard the voices of the women, waging their war against the summer in the street: He doesn't hear, no, he simply doesn't hear... oh, I could just throw myself into the lake! And their voices made the sickle moon tremble, thin as a thread, a symbol of remote, unearthly elegance floating in the east above the black woods.

As by day, my nightly path took me to a small peninsula that jutted omega-shaped into a secluded forest lake. The narrow causeway leading out to the head of the formation—a dam that regularly vanished, inundated, in the spring; only a line of trees rose from the water to show where it lay, and the reed-edged circle of marsh in the middle of the lake was a true island—this path leading out was so densely flanked by brush and birch saplings that you vanished from sight the moment you set foot on it. At night the gleaming birch leaves caught the moonlight, and when they stirred in a breeze, a flutter or flicker passed down the edge of the causeway, an iridescent glitter like crinkled tinfoil, coming from beyond, from the rubbish heaps that loomed nearby forbiddingly with the blood-red light of fires, hellfires, shooting up between them: the red luminescence and the moon's silver dazzle were echoed in the ripples of the bay, shifting out and back again, until the glimmer was swallowed by a cloud's shadow-flight... and the shadow-form groping its way through birch thickets out onto the lake had not failed to note the cloud. Directly above the circular island, straight up from the head of the omega, the cloud stopped, so it seemed, to cast down its darkness: the sharp shadow of the cloud beneath the moon fell upon the marshy isle and shrouded it completely; the inner circle of the reed girdle immediately went dark ... blotted out, lightless beneath the cloud, a place of utter invisibility: here you could learn unbeing through sheer being, here you could wait out the night. It was virtually shut out, the night that lay upon the lake, resting and yet restlessly at work, perpetually processing secrets like a ruminant beast; there was always some stir in the tall, impenetrable reeds that girded the peninsula: a constant moan and sigh in the growing of the reeds, as though night sought an answer there ... some word from the invisible things that kept hidden in the dark.

No! I said. No, they could be glad if I came back before dawn, if they found me in bed in the morning. They could be content if I held my tongue in the face of their remonstrances. If I made no comment, positive or negative, on their suspicion that I'd been gone all night; they could be happy if my reaction to their reproaches—my renewed disappearance—was possible only once the day was done, when they themselves might already be sleeping. Earlier, when I was just eight or ten, I'd known how to confront them, I'd raised my own voice, screaming too: I'm not coming, no, no! I'll never come ... not back here! I won't stay, I don't want to, I don't have to, I don't want to have to anymore! — And their reply was the shrieked-out announcement that they'd throw themselves into the lake. It had its effect, I fled, I escaped out to the rubbish dumps, to the lake, and again and again my path led across to the peninsula, by sun or by rain; even when I heard their voices grow fainter, more broken, spoken half to the floor, toward some pale specter crouched in a forlorn corner; they called to me so voicelessly that I could forego protest.

Yet I continued to seek the stillness I found on the

peninsula: perhaps they murmured on when I was out there, perhaps the words rose quite unthinking from their lips, like the barely-visible thread of smoke that falls from a snuffed candle's wick. Or only they themselves now heard what they had once said, like an incomprehensible echo, resounding back from the dungeon of the last years, and they themselves could no longer understand their own words.

For me, however, their cries were always present, ushering me and goading me on; they'd lodged in my ear, perhaps forever, intolerable music, either hastening or choking my breath. At night they could be heard from afar—as though the neighbors' sons were beating their wives—and from town the moaning drew an arc through the sky; I huddled behind the reeds and watched the wisps of mist drifting over the lake, and they too seemed to listen; I thought I saw a glimmering white, flimsy form among them, pausing on a boat washed by the black waves . . . a form that held intently still, as though the half-faded lament strove forth from my brain, its locus, to entrust itself to the ears of the mist—they reared up straight so as not to miss what lay behind the sound of the waves splashing into the reeds. — And suddenly I recalled a great mudhole, right in the center of the island, where we had sunned ourselves as children.

I recalled the sinful sense of well-being that came over me when I stripped off my clothes to stretch out in the thick black mud that filled the bottom of the hollow. It was a grainy slurry of coal slack and sand in burnt-smelling water, whose surface, when smooth, showed yellow striations of sulfur. In this puddle I lay every afternoon of the endless summer, when the mud was very warm, sometimes almost hot; the oblong hole held the whole of my body, I ceased to move and waited until at last stillness came over me. Eyes nearly shut, I stared up into a sky whose rim was ablaze, and where the sun, straight above me, was an indistinct circle of white heat from which, now and then, a drop seemed to fall . . . and a yellow cloud, nearly white, seemed to draw near this sun, touching the edge of its glaring gorge and beginning to melt.

Raindrops fell, a steaming yellow rain from the sun-hot sky, moisture that burned in the eyes. The sun-rain increased, the liquid in the mud puddle rose, the slurry that penetrated all my folds, all my pores, closed smoothly over my thighs; it rained harder, seething floods poured from a sky almost fully blue, the mud rose higher, hot and sucking it closed over my protruding sex, crept oppressively up my belly and my chest, and I waited tensely for it to reach my neck; already my arms were firmly embedded in the tenacious black tide that forced its relentless way up to my armpits, pressing my shoulders to the bottom, so that I seemed to merge inseparably with the peaty soil. Already I felt a terrifying tickle beneath my chin, and sensed my hair growing into the swamp below me, as though to root my body in the earth. And I seemed to have utterly dissolved in a black heat, the light of the sky still blinding me behind closed lids, as the rain splashed in the mud on my chest and boiled all about on the water of the lake, as dried stubs of plants softened and began to steam foully, as the rain crackled and rustled in the reeds as though to break them down or erect them . . . and under the weight of the seething vapors all around something shot out from my body, something like a dull pain, something hard within me that had dissolved and turned liquid, departing me with monstrous ease, only my loins had flared and faded once more, only a brief rearing and stretching of my trapped spine, and I was still again, suddenly soft and unfeeling, nothing now but rot and water, indistinguishable from the elements around me and above me with which I had mingled myself.

In that moment the shrill song in my ears broke off. From then on the scolding and the threats fell still; there was a silence within me, as though the cries wished to be mere memory; gradually I began to forget them. — *Into the lake... into the lake*, the women's venting utterance seemed suddenly to have gone mute. And at once I began to miss it; a moment later I felt that, from this time on, I would have to seek the voices of the women.

In secret I eyed their closed mouths, which seemed pinched and gray, oddly blurred and colorless; they wasted no more words on my unseemly behavior: on my coming too late, not coming at all... oh, my coming had ceased to matter to them. And so they no longer promised to go, go throw themselves into the lake... they ceased to threaten me with it, and stayed where they were. There was a dully flowing, yellow-green veil between us, made of rain, made of mist, and all words and retorts were lost in it. We no longer reached the surface; a chill prevailed between us, inevitably seeping inside if we offered even the tiniest opening.

It was pointless now to avow how I loved them, pointless to concede what they had once extorted, the irrefutable proof of my love, the liquid proof of my love that would encompass them all... and that I no longer had the strength to mobilize in myself. In all the years that had sunk from my reach I had sought to hoard the names of love within me, a river of names, a deluge of words, a swell of endearments frothing and mounting . . . I couldn't find them, or the words failed to find *me*. They, the women they were meant for, were too old for them, I had missed the right moment. The names of love had bailed out somewhere, crossed over to an unknown shore, they were on the far edge of a bleak river, out of my reach, scattered and barren like dim stars above my smoking nights.

But one last time I resolved to follow them: the words of the women, or my words, or their silence, or mine. I set out in search of what seemed lost to me. Again I left the house in the middle of the night and wandered for a long time, breathing heavily I strayed through the liquid moonlight: I recalled the mudhole from my childhood . . . Perhaps it was there, I thought, that I lost everything! — I hastened through woods where wafts of mist fooled my eyes, like nightgowns fleeing, then over an open field, across the endless rubbish heaps where the empty bottles and flickering snakes of tinfoil echoed the unearthly gleam of the sickle moon, and where deep in the night came a dark red glow as from subterranean fires. At last I found the peninsula, the omega: already I saw myself from afar, running across amid the thickets to the center of the island . . . the birches had grown tall, the underbrush thin, but the trees were bare, they had died and rotted, their crumbling trunks soaked with water. I reached the shore and saw the lake stretched between the dark ruined trees, the causeway lay under water; it was impossible now to cross to the island, looming from the waves before the fiery glow like the fragment of a skull whose hair stood on end. And at a distance drifted clumps of foam—or were they clots of fog?—some of them erect, twisting upward like rising spirals, or like ghosts circling the island in wobbling boats . . .

Not yet, ferryman, I said, I'm not ready to board your boat. Cast off once more without me, old friend; I must find my way back first. I must know those names first, that myriad of names . . . then I'll follow you.

For one day I will find them . . . and then, to show you all, I'll hurl it after you, my love, and the names for it, and the thoughts I have. — Into the lake! The lake! I cried, and, inflamed by a dull bolt of lightning in my body, I stepped close to the shore, where I tore my trousers open. Panting I began to empty myself, as though to form a bond between myself and the earth, I pissed steaming into the water, pain-fully I poured myself and emptied myself utterly into the dark water on which the swelling white gowns floated.

THE SLEEP OF THE RIGHTEOUS

The dark divests us of our qualities. — Though we breathe more greedily, struggling for life, for some fleeting web of substance from the darkness . . . it is the darkness that forms a mute block above us: intangible matter our breaths cannot lighten . . . it seems to burst apart at each answer from the old man, each lament of his breath, yet sinks in again swiftly to weigh down still closer, in the cohesive calm of myriad tiny black, gyrating viruses. And we rest one whole long night in this block of black viruses, we rest from the toils of the day: from the everyday toil of circling each other, still and hostile. By day we keep silent, we know too much about ourselves, and our resolve to skirt or ignore this knowledge of ourselves is unshakeable. For years no contention has arisen between us, it seems settled that we respect both our lives, that we grant ourselves our existence. His existence is that of the father of his daughter, mine that of the son of my mother, no more and no less; the woman we mean, descendant of a dead woman, sleeps in more distant back rooms. One of our qualities, common to both of us, must be an arduously hidden fear: never mentioned in the light, it exhausts us in night sweats, swallowed by the dark, which we put down to the hot summer nights. We rest sweating side by side in an old marriage bed, and the square weight of the gloom lies upon us, clasps us, it presses us together, we lie with bodies completing each other, like two conspirators exchanging signs with their breaths.

When Grandmother died, it was decided without discussion that I, still a child, would move that same day to her vacated bed, next to my grandfather, so as to banish for good all clarity as to who had killed the old woman. And he, the old man, parted that day from his daughter... she retired to the back, into my former room.

It was one of us two, that much is for sure: it was a blow from the cast-iron poker, descending with a thud to strike her on the hip, right between kidney and spine, a blow to which, after weeks of hunched shuffling and vomiting of black blood, she ultimately succumbed. How absurd that her end was ascribed to several prunes, soaked in cold water, which she was said to have eaten too greedily; it was the farcical justification that we had all agreed to believe, and no one dared call it a cowardly fiction.

He who goes to bed first is the innocent one, for he can fall asleep. If the old man goes first, if he's asleep already when I come, the strained, sustained groaning and snoring that rises from his rib cage won't let me fall asleep, not until I grasp at last, hours later perhaps, its irregular rhythm, and am able in the pauses in which he seems to have died, so long and so stunned are they, to chime in with my own groans and snores, so that our two voices begin to prowl about each other. They seek to wear each other down in a continual game of questions and answers that suddenly breaks free of its confusion and becomes a game in which at synchronized intervals we accuse each other again and again. — *Who? Whoo* . . . is the ever-repeated question concealed within one of these chest tones; and: *You! Youu* . . . is the response that just as inevitably follows.

Sometimes I awaken with a start, bathed with sweat in a darkness that admits no concept of time, and even before I completely come to, the last of his emphatic replies enters my still-feeble consciousness so fiercely that I turn rigid with dread. For a moment, he seems to listen, but my wheezing question doesn't come; he tosses with sinister force onto his other side, turning toward me, I can't tell if his eyes are open, and before I can place the horror of that insistent *you* in my vaguely straying thoughts, I've fallen asleep again; he turns back onto the old side, I feel his back at my breast again, again we lie like the nested forms of two soup spoons, my hand once more touching his. And I feel how, full of fury, he awaits the judgment from my howling throat; over and over, with the tirelessness of a torturer, he'll ask me the terrible question: *Whoo . . . ?* — *Youu . . . !* I'll reply. *Whooo . . .* — *Youuu . . .* — And so on, and it seems that sleep is assured to me till morning. It seems we both believe firmly in the reciprocal truth of our testimony.

But in reality we've both forgotten the true course of events, and we both think ourselves the murderer. Or both of us doubt that the murderer was the other. It's a circling about a common guilt, it's two ellipses of a double guilt no longer to be teased apart; night after night it grows menacingly into the dark and drives the viruses of the gloom into a frenzy. No doubt the survivor will be the murderer... whichever of us two dies first will sink redeemed into his grave... no doubt that's why we hold our breath so often and so long. — The survivor, suddenly isolated, suddenly lacking his consort, lacking his accuser by his side, will fully grasp his guilt: while the innocent one sleeps forever, the guilty one shall never taste sleep again. Long, grinding thoughts will keep him awake... the initiate with the power to keep silent is dead. The powerless one is left behind; fear will torment him, mistrust of all the neighbors whose unrest he senses more keenly in the short summer nights, when his voice can be heard through the open window on the street: how much longer can the preposterous tale of the prunes be maintained? There is no one left who knows when the plum trees in the garden were felled; when might someone ask whether that wasn't before the old woman's death?

Bad dreams will visit the survivor's doze; at one point he'll think his grandfather has come in; while he feigns sleep, the old man will turn his back, drop his trousers to his knees, seat the lean, unsightly bareness of his buttocks on the bed, shed his trousers all the way, and lie beside him with a groan, hands folded on his breast in the innocent hope of sleep... meanwhile the one left behind will wrench his eyes open all the way and see that he's alone. — Never again will they nestle against each other by turns, one's back pressed to the other's front, filling all the bends of the sideways position, hands clawed together, dealing out each other's breaths, rhythmic in heat and gloom. — Again and again the survivor will dream the first day of solitude, dreaming every night anew the horror with which, waking, he grasps that his last question has gone without a reply... until he hears the reply from the depths of his own breast: none but he can be meant, beside him the bed is abandoned.

Now the summer nights grow shorter and fiercer, his groaning and snoring hectic and ever louder, increasingly perturbed that the whole street, and the side streets as well, hear him circle himself with his indictments, hear him talk in his sleep, struggling for life and yet cursing himself, unable as he is to follow the old man into innocence.

The woman in her distant room knows nothing of all this... and is my initiate all the same; she bore me and abandoned me to this hideously long life. She slumbers for me, all the deeper since I've grown up out of childhood. She's oblivious of the cycle of the viruses, oblivious that close at hand the world's guilt dreams of vengeance—one day I'll move the block of night, one day I must roll it over her body.

THE AFTERNOON

Nothing new on Bahnhofstrasse! — These are the first words to occur to me upon arrival. With the word *arrival*, though, I've already said too much: there's something so familiar in the soapy taste of the air that I wouldn't dream of describing my walk into town as a return—I don't think of myself coming back; I've never been away. No, I never really left the town, sometimes I fled it, that's all: in truth it was the town that never really left me. The town took me over with its drab devastation, in which some perpetually stalled upheaval seemed in progress, an inexplicable upheaval. I always had this impression, long before the whole country's upheaval, and it lingered after the country's authorities had surrendered and fled, after the government and its closest vassals had been replaced: this town seemed in no way to confirm the changing of the system. In a past apparently impossible to fathom now, the town must have plunged into paralysis, and that collapse had survived the regime change.

For years I fled from the town, years that have sped from my grasp as though chased by the furies, and yet never passed quickly enough for me. These are all the years I can recall with ease, quite in contrast to those I spent here in this town. It's as though in those other cities, the bigger, more attractive ones I chose to live in, I never really settled down. Those cities' easily summoned images were dimmed by a sense of loss, a sentimental feeling originating in this town to which I return from time to time. It's here that this barely explicable sense of absence grew on me, one I only really felt once I had settled down elsewhere with the more or less firm resolution to stay. It made itself felt as a kind of living without a background, it was a state of severance, a state without a past, and yet I'd learned to feel severed from the past in the small town afternoons.

Time persisted here in dogged immutability; the autumnal fog banks that merged beneath an earth-colored sky appeared unlikely to pass for decades to come. And more and more smoke seemed to spill from the sodden lowlands into the flat clouds, which, even in the afternoon, were nocturnal.

Nothing new in the town of M., then. — Bahnhofstrasse, the station road, is still rutted by construction pits, as it was months before, the last time I came here: in the same darkness in which gusts of wind seem to snatch the faint light from the trembling lamps that mark, at irregular intervals, the edge of what was once the sidewalk. Cold fog with wind and rain knotted in it; now snow seems to mingle there as well. The way ahead of me has metamorphosed into a causeway of shadow, beginning to glitter treacherously. Ahead of me hurry a few bundled-up people who got off the train along with me; the street seems barely negotiable, on both sides the invisible looms. I look about for a better path: the alternative route is also broken up and blocked by railings behind which, in the yellow-red flicker of lamps, listing construction vehicles seem to sink into the sand. Every route has been torn up; evidently, after digging up half the town, all work was ceased; I've never known it to be otherwise.

For one fleeting moment—an eddy of wind parts the mix of rain and snow—I can see the clock on the station façade: it shows three! — There's no mistake, it always told this time, its hands always formed this exact right angle in the upper part of the dial: three o'clock, as long as I can remember. I have a photograph a friend took of me at the lower end of Bahnhofstrasse, twenty or more years ago. Our intention was to record the strange sight of a bulky pipeline: along the side façades of the factory buildings by the road, the pipe, more than a yard in diameter with its insulation, ran straight across the factory windows, blocking both the view and the daylight, so that the lights in the factory halls had to be left on perpetually. The spectacle of this disconcerting stopgap constituted the charm of the photograph for us; it recalled some absurd technological fantasy. — The station stood at the street's upper end: on the clearly discernable clock above its entrance it was precisely three o'clock!

Eternal afternoon prevails in the town. The photo shows not a soul on the sharply lit street; the trees, evidently sycamores, still in existence then, are bare. Beneath the white-gray autumn sky, the town has been struck by some blow of mysterious origin. At exactly three o'clock on an ice-cold Sunday, when none of the inhabitants were on the street, the town had been transformed into a phantasm. It had frozen to a motionless backdrop; no one noticed, not even that harmless hobby photographer, himself observed only from behind

grimy curtains by several perpetually lurking informers. —
Ever since then you were excluded, upon entering the city,
from a fundamental law of human existence: since then you
were excluded from the soft, relentless onward flow of time,
which the trigger of an old-fashioned camera had brought to
a standstill. There was only one copy of this black and white
photo; the negative had vanished in the dusty back rooms of
a photo lab whose owner retired long ago.

And ever since then you were transformed into a shadow
upon entering this town, this sinister, bleakly motley heap of
houses. And if someone had walked the streets at night, only
years later might you hear his steps echoing up the walls.

Those were my thoughts when I'd walked across town
and sat at last in my little upstairs kitchen. I thought of these
steps, scuffing, hasty, sometimes dragging with weariness,
and I thought that they had never ceased . . . they were the
only movement in the town. — Outside, human life and living voices still existed! Beyond the bounds of this obliterated
town I sensed language still at work, and I believed that with
its help certain things could be achieved. New generations
will partake of it, I told myself; I'd long been waiting for the
moment when young people would at last take on the language. And at last seize the ideas buried in the language, and
put them on the line. Perhaps I myself had grown unable to
guess at these ideas; for far too long now, words have seemed
to give out on me. But in some obscure future perhaps the
words will reemerge, I thought. Like lights that flicker and
stutter at first, as when long-forgotten wires and connections
are suddenly flooded with electricity.

I've always spoken of the wrong things, presumably! At

least that was my perpetual suspicion...and despite my change of scenery, I increasingly felt I was governed by inertia. Inertia kept me captive, lying constantly in wait, prepared to take full possession of me, to fix me like a botched statue to the spot where I happened to be. — The cause lies here in M., I said to myself. Here, in this town, annihilation planted its foot on me. — And how long ago was it that I began to dissect the doom I called M. into words and phrases in order to achieve clarity about it: how many years ago that I failed in the attempt and gave up again...

When I visited the town of M., all I wanted was to return as soon as possible to a burning lamp over a kitchen table in a tiny, smoke-filled, eat-in kitchen familiar from my childhood. It had two windows facing the yard, and, on the other walls, peeling, blistered, yellow wallpaper displaying a peculiar pattern under the shadow of its discolorations: at first glance one had the impression that lines of dark brown vermin were marching straight up the walls. When I'd heated the coal stove, the wallpaper seemed to sweat, emitting the nicotine lodged in its pores since the beginning of eternity. The windows had warped in the damp; I'd used old towels to block the cold that seeped in at their edges. If possible, I left the lamp over the table burning all the time; its wires were heavily oxidized, porous. Dating back before the war, they refused to conduct electricity when switched on and off too often, and only protracted manipulation of the contacts could start the current flowing again. — In this old cave—in this relic from the early twentieth century—I sat and turned my pages, covered with crossed-out or not yet crossed-out lines. Instead of writing, I smoked cigarette after cigarette and listened to the darkness that hung inert outside the windows. There was nothing to be heard...I couldn't hear a thing, all sounds were swallowed by the enervating whine of the ancient refrigerator, whose unstable power unit kept starting up at far-too-brief intervals.

My reflections on this town had likely begun at a time now lost in mythic twilight. Indeed I had tried, again and again, to form a picture of the town which, if I was not mistaken, was still out there, which probably still clustered around my lighted interior, frozen and stony and hollow. I had even persuaded myself that this was my sole purpose... and perhaps for that very reason it had become for me a senseless, useless undertaking. Often I believed that first I had to invent the town by describing it...perhaps it could come into existence in no other way. The fact that I had been born in it was not sufficient to prove its existence...

How can one demand of a shadow that he describe the image of a shadow town? — It was absurd questions like that I grappled with. And a long-familiar effect had taken hold: my goal, the image of the town, seemed to recede still further from me each time I believed, thanks to blind chance, that I'd come closer for a moment...the goal sought to evade me! I was accordingly ill-disposed toward my endeavor. — But perhaps there did exist, somewhere in the streets, a certain shadow for whom such an image was possible... weren't there footsteps in the depths of town, padding steps I strained my ears after? First they had receded, but now they returned again. Weren't those steps down on the pavement the proof I was seeking? I listened a long time, hour after hour, but there was not much to hear, due to the refrigerator noise—a central, recurring motif brought to me by the run-down things of the twentieth century—which constantly drowned everything out. And the light began to flicker, for seconds at a time, each time the refrigerator switched itself on.

How can you sit calmly at a table and write, I said to myself, and set down the impression of a completely inert town, when you're constantly tormented by the knowledge that someone out there in the dark is being hunted, and may this very moment be running for his life?

However frightful the deluge of refrigerator noise: I seemed to keep hearing those hasty steps out on the street. From the moment I arrived in M. I was unable to escape the thought. The door to the next room, with the street window, stood ajar, and I heard the clatter and shuffle of well-worn shoes on the crooked stones of the sidewalk. First it was a single person's steps; soon I thought several others were following him. After a while the single steps returned, and sometimes they strayed into the yard, sometimes coming right beneath the two kitchen windows between which I sat, listening in horror. In a moment I could expect him to call my name... I stood up and extinguished the light. Once I felt safe, I turned the lamp on again: of course it wouldn't burn; I climbed onto the table, lighting my way with the cigarette lighter, and jiggled the cable until the two fluorescent tubes shone once more. The whole thing repeated until my thoughts were in tatters: that crackling and flaring, and then again the slackening steps, once it had grown still.

Sometimes it ceased, but the hunt in the streets was far from over. He had managed to shake them only temporarily.

It seemed he'd hidden himself in a dark corner; my yard served in a pinch to let his pursuers pass by. But all he got was a breathing spell; soon they tracked him down again. They were long since wise to all his ruses, they'd been after him for years; I would have had to count back to say when this story had begun. There was no reason for it...no one out there knew any reason. — And often enough they caught him, presumably they could catch him at their whim. At any time they could corner him and let him run into a trap: he was one man, there were always more of them, they took turns, they could increase their force at will.

I recall all too well how once, in the very beginning, when their malice was still boundless—a few weeks, in other words, after setting their sights on him—they had snatched him off the street and beaten him horribly. It was a winter night, between three and four in the morning, when I heard a voice calling softly outside the kitchen windows and thought I could make out my name. With the last of his strength he'd dragged himself into my yard, where he collapsed in the slush. I had to help him up the stairs; evidently he could hardly see. I helped him lie down on the sofa in the kitchen and administered several shots of liquor. His lips were split, blood dripped from his nose. Both eyes had swelled nearly shut, and shards from his glasses were embedded in his lacerated brows, clearly due to a blow from a truncheon. I tried to get some explanation out of him, but he merely hissed out profanities and curses; he murmured on even after falling asleep.

Not long after this scene he was sent to prison for a year; on his release his papers bore a stamp authorizing him to cross the border. He had three days to leave the country; together we went around to the authorities, whom neither of us cared to visit, to gather the signatures he needed, attesting, among other things, that he'd paid his electric bills, had no outstanding library books, and had taken care of the fee for clearing out his cellar. An hour before his departure we packed his belongings, filling barely half of an olive canvas duffel bag. In the afternoon I accompanied him to the last bus to the district capital, which he had to take to catch the interzonal train to Frankfurt am Main that would bring him across the border before midnight. I refused to believe that he was glad to go. We were silent for most of the way to the bus station, or at least we didn't speak of how he was leaving the country with no real conviction, and no precise notion what his destination was. He was limping, but insisted on carrying the bag himself; though it weighed nearly nothing, it pulled his slender shoulders askew. Before boarding the bus, he turned his face to me, now pale, and said he'd never set foot in this country again. — You've got no other choice, I thought, but didn't say it out loud; I saw him sitting behind the grimed bus window, staring stoically straight ahead. There was no point in waving again, for as the bus drove off, I saw that his eyes were closed behind his thick lenses; an inscrutable smile played about his lips.

Just a few days later I could have sworn I saw his duffle bag again. I happened to walk down the street where he'd lived, and saw it lying on the sill of the ground floor window, which had never had curtains. I'd often worked myself up about that: he offered an unobstructed view through his window to every sewer rat and every belly-worm employed by the state apparatus. It was all the same to him. — I knocked on the pane; nothing stirred, so I went into the building and hammered on the door of his flat: no one answered; his name plate had been removed from the front door.

Revenge! Revenge, I thought, it could only be revenge that they'd wanted. — But revenge for what? — I still sought an explanation for the story, but there was no chance for an explanation. At any rate, there were always enough people to put together a posse! There were policemen and secret police-men, and any number of overzealous little snitches who would have given anything to play Inspector Maigret. Who even did it free of charge, just to show how much they cared about law and order in this town. How many humble citizens with windows on the street took up their posts behind the curtains at the least unusual noise? I couldn't imagine that, of all their traits, this one might have changed.

And yet my friend wasn't even a homosexual or a Jew, he wore his hair only moderately long, and he had no car to commit a parking violation. He was only a humble chem-ist who'd quit his job at the factory because he was over-qualified, and since then stayed afloat by repairing TV sets; word had gotten out that he did a better job than the official service company. He spent his spare time in his tiny apart-ment, hunched over inscrutable chemical formulas, painting abstract pictures, or developing his own amateur photos. Now and then he'd drink a drop too much. The anonymous letters about him received by a certain section of the munici-pal council described nocturnal gatherings in his apartment that went on into the morning. I had attended several of those gatherings; the way they talked about literature and music put me in a foul mood, and I went home early.

Now, when I walked past his former apartment, I looked back wistfully on those discussions; my arrogance has long since fled. The little discussion groups had scattered soon after his expulsion. And they had never come back together again, not even now... even less so now, in the time after the system's collapse, when it actually would have been possible: today there seemed not a person left in town who talked voluntarily about literature. Only the others, literature's adversaries, had remained. They hunkered behind the haze of their curtains and kept the street under surveillance. But there was no one down there who was not of their ilk.

I had never succeeded in describing the town. Neither from up close nor from afar; I simply hadn't found a way to look at it, I saw that more and more clearly. — It was he who could have pulled off this description, and in his own way, though quite unintentionally, he had pulled it off. This was what I thought when I passed by his window, behind which he was often seen puttering around; now curtains hung against the polished panes, and inside a TV flickered murkily. My friend had merely released the shutter of his camera one cold fall Sunday, and the snapshot produced at that moment had unmasked the town. Three o'clock: at precisely that second the town had frozen to an image of black and white lifelessness. And they had been after him ever since. — Maybe they're only after the photo, I thought. If they got it, would they leave him in peace? — But I never really believed that.

I knew what awaited me in M.; I'd given up all hope

for change. When I got off the rickety suburban train and crossed the station hall, already seeing several odd, loitering figures who took a striking interest in the bare walls when I passed, and when I walked down Bahnhofstrasse and turned further down onto the main street, not without looking about to see whether I was being followed in due form, then I knew that nothing had changed here. By the marketplace, at the latest, I ceased to care whether they were following me; I knew I was now in the past, in a time that hadn't moved from the spot. I'd been unable to make out the station clock, but I was convinced that its hands hadn't moved an iota. Fog, drizzle, and snow sank unchanged through the islands of reddish streetlights, as though even the weather were a mere expression of stagnation and the past. When I arrived in my kitchen at last, when the fluorescent tubes burned over the table, when the stove was heated, I spread out my papers in front of me. And as my perplexity grew, I began listening to the night outside.

Now and then I thought I heard steps down in the street: he, he alone could describe the town, but he didn't, at least not as I would have done. — He was the restless spirit of this town, his presence spectral and indisputable. And when he thought about the town, it was in phrases that came ever faster, ever shorter; short-winded phrases; meanwhile he passed without pausing. They were after him, as they were every night. He fled, began to limp, I could hear it clearly; he was already flagging. He didn't stop, he went on to the end of the street. There he disappeared, but only for a moment. He could think the town's story only in fits and starts, without patience, without beginning and end.

More and more often he stopped to catch his breath, pressing himself into an entryway, listening into the darkness. He knew they were there somewhere, listening as well. A little further. At the next corner he set down the olive-drab bag and asked a chance passerby for a light. The cigarette glowed in his cupped hand, and he walked on. After just a few steps he threw away the cigarette and ran. He came past the train station, skirting it, straight through the wet shrubs, then slid down a railroad embankment and returned to town via muddy side streets, as he'd often done before. But he couldn't shake them off; they were always somewhere in the darkness behind him. At some point the church clock on the market square struck, like the reverberation of a second that had slipped into a coma. I counted the strokes, he did not; he ran on.

The photo he had taken years before was in my possession, and really it was *I* they should have hunted.

THE MEMORIES

It was an odd thing: in the night, the dark morning, he'd feel driven out onto the street again. — How should he call it: a habit, a restlessness from former times that had grown old with him? He wanted no more part of it! — For instance, he'd walk up the street to the mailbox at this ungodly hour, as he'd taken to calling it. And he knew that he was trying to avoid meeting any of the people who set out this early, between four and five, on their daily way to work. It was long since C. had been one of them, more than fifteen years, but down on the dark street, on the maybe five hundred yards to the mailbox, it was clear to him that a disquiet from that time still lay deep within. This disquiet was otherwise silent, he was quite immune to the thought of it, but at that particular hour something within him responded ... Quite automatically! he said to himself.

A single stumble, and that old feeling resurfaced: he was driven by the duty to set out into the world, and yet he didn't want to. He wasn't even able yet to let himself be driven. In a daze he watched himself charge onward, coughing, sucking at a cigarette; the cold made his eyes water, he felt the icy runnels on his cheeks. The frosty air blew every bit of sleep from his brain, but his thoughts refused to clear, nothing but numbness was left in his skull. The frozen block behind his brow held but one aspiration: to reach the station in time, to drop onto the red-brown plastic upholstery of the dimly lit railcar, and there, for precisely eight minutes, amidst relative warmth, to collapse.

He had to get out at the very next station. There was another stretch of road before him, still more unpleasant, as it led through the open terrain of the mine pits. The wind howled here, raising sharp, icy dust from the road's concrete slabs and flinging it into his face. But somehow he always seemed to have soaked up warmth in the suburban train, making the stretch to the factory entrance easier to cover.

Now, on the short trip to the mailbox, he felt abruptly transformed to a previous state: all that had befallen him in his later life, all that had changed him, suddenly seemed unreal, a way of life forced upon him by whim or by chance, for which there was no real inward reason. Now he was every bit the half-stupefied figure from back then, hastening onwards, coattails flying, beneath the wind-rattled lamps. He hurried through their circles of orange light that scattered, shifting across the pavement. In many places this pavement was uneven, bulging and split as though something pressed on it from underneath. And he often thought these places changed overnight, and kept tripping him unexpectedly; and each time his feet caught on the crooked slabs, a strange sentence came into his mind: I don't need to know what's down there beneath me!

He remembered: he'd already had a restless spell

yesterday. Just after four, before the need for sleep came over him, the long-familiar emptiness gaped within, as it regularly did; if he hadn't yet been to the mailbox, he'd pull on his coat over the faded old sweat suit he wore in the house, slip on his shoes, usually without socks, and run outside with his shoelaces untied. The street was usually deserted; it would have been awkward for him to run into someone he knew in his slipshod get-up. Only a few cars would pass him, headlights on full beam, and for a few seconds he'd jog along in their light; doubtless no one recognized him, he'd left town long ago.

They raced down the street as though hopelessly late. — Those who still had work, and that wasn't many these days, might have driven off an hour ago already; it seemed they commuted to jobs in Bavaria, in Hof or even Nuremberg, driving hundreds of kilometers, spending up to fifteen hours away from home each day. Of course, they earned twice what they could have at the few jobs here. And here they paid much less rent. But they were hardly ever home; despite the money, their marriages broke up one by one.

He sometimes had half a mind to mention these things in the letters he sent. He had this urge each time he got a letter from West Germany sharing someone's evident gratification at how the East German towns were finally being refurbished.

There you have it, he thought, now they're replastering the façades, and bit by bit the former Zone's houses will cease to offend West German eyes.

In actual fact, he wrote nothing of the sort; generally, when people adopted such a tone, he let the correspondence lapse quite quickly. The messages he sent consisted of just a few inconsequential lines, often addressed to people he barely knew even in passing. — He'd write to them that he had to remember, or at least thought he had to, because the town he came from, where he'd grown up, essentially no longer existed, and his memories of this place had turned porous, with more and more holes gaping in them.

It sounded like an attempt to justify his frequent visits to the small town where his mother still lived. No one whosoever had asked. And yet he volunteered replies; his letters and postcards were composed of evasive, overcautious replies to questions no one had asked, making the whole thing even more mysterious: it seemed he was merely answering his own questions. It astonished him that he couldn't find a self-evident reason to visit the house where he was born, that coming to town to see his mother wasn't reason enough.

What am I actually trying to remember? he'd ask himself, back from the mailbox. — In the old days I'd have had to get up an hour ago to report punctually for the life I barely recall now. — His mother had had to wake him each morning, and by the time he appeared in the as-yet unheated kitchen, which still smelled of his cigarettes from the night before, she would have the coffee ready. — Then we sat facing each other in silence; I drank my two cups of coffee while she waited for me to make it out the door. For years, at that ungodly hour, we were this taciturn, tight-lipped couple, sunk in our separate worlds. And shut away within, we probably held the knowledge of all the nameless generations before us that had sat just like this in the dark winter mornings, man and woman, waiting mute and servile for the urgent start of the workday to part them: my grandfather had occupied this place, and then she'd sat this way with her husband, my father, and after that it was the same thing with me; it seemed an inescapable fate. — C. asked himself at times how many memories were sealed within her, in the withered, forbidding old woman's body from which nothing emerged to the outside.

He'd feel warmth again only once he passed the watchman, when he'd crossed the dark yard of frozen grass behind the administrative building and reported to the boiler room, which was located beneath the showers and changing rooms. Only after taking over from the night shift would the frost leave his limbs and warmth return to his unfeeling face. — The night shift was a scrawny, somber individual who answered to the name of Gunsch; his first name was unknown, forgotten because it couldn't be pronounced, and as no one called him by it, perhaps he himself had long since forgotten it. Even his time card bore only the handwritten name *Gunsch*. He came from a town the other way down the railroad tracks, an old Pole who, it was claimed, had been pensioned off some unknown number of years ago and pursued his job in the boiler room for no reason but avarice. But these claims ignored the fact that at the start of each winter the factory had to talk him into postponing his retirement for one more heating period. It was nearly impossible to find workers to man this old, outlying factory wing; most of the people working here were indisputably in banishment. Production Area 6 was the official name of the steep bluff that jutted, a spit of earth seemingly spared by chance, into the foggy void of the mine pits . . . on whose tip, next to a disused, derelict, red-brick briquette plant, a new production hall had been constructed, painted green, with glass walls that made it nearly impossible to heat... This factory wing, this last loose fang in the lost dentures of the workers' and peasants' state, was the workplace of the delinquents, the alcoholics, and those who had rebelled against the factory hierarchy, people, in other words, who had to be sent out of sight.

When C. came to relieve him, Gunsch was ready and waiting in his street clothes; their color and cut differed little from his work clothes, but now his neck and head were muffled with scarves and a military-looking leather cap with earflaps. His little face showed shadows of coal dust and ash that the water of the shower could not dispel, and the color of the coal had eaten its way into his chapped hands. He pointed his stubby black finger around the boiler room, mumbling incomprehensible explanations; C. nodded pro forma agreement to everything, and at last the old man vanished. C. climbed back up the stairs from the boiler room to stamp his colleague's time card in the factory hall; his card had been marked by Gunsch half an hour ago with the wrong arrival time. As day broke, one saw the old man riding his ramshackle bicycle into the fog and the ice. On barely detectable paths along the railroad tracks, he pedaled away between the chasms of the mine pits; each time one wondered when the ground in front of him would peter out into nothingness and this strange black bird, forced to flap up from the treacherous terrain, would rise into the air.

When Gunsch spoke, no one could understand a word, but that was all right, for he rarely said anything of a communicative nature. No one knew exactly how and where he lived, what he did with his money, whether he even kept human company outside working hours. There was a persistent legend that he dwelled in the midst of the mine pits, in a house without electricity, cut off from the outside world, his farmstead all that remained of a tiny village that had been bulldozed because it stood atop the coal. In the middle of his garden the ground broke off into the depths, said those who claimed to have seen it; of course most of the stories told in Factory Wing 6, the raving drunkards' wing, were wildly exaggerated. He bought his necessities at the factory's little store, wrapped them up in burlap and transported them on his bicycle rack out into the no-man's-land from which he hadn't set foot since the end of the war. At some point in the unfathomable years of his life he had come here from the *East*—the direction alone seemed to convey enough about that blurrily bounded region from which C.'s grandfather had also immigrated at the turn of the century. At any rate, the German Gunsch spoke was laid waste in a way C. knew from his grandfather. Due to these putatively shared origins, he had begun to take an interest in the old Pole. Gunsch regarded all attempts at understanding as pointless from the outset. When he opened his mouth, he seemed to spout only curses, and no one in the boiler room knew the exact object of this abuse.

Of course, proper German was no requirement for the backbreaking work of the boiler room. It sufficed that he could fill the iron coal wagon, which loomed taller than his alarmingly narrow shoulders, about eight or nine times every four hours, quickly enough that pressure would build up in all four boilers at once, sending the steam all the way back into the new factory hall. A bag of bones like Gunsch, the stokers claimed, actually had an easier time of it in the cramped coal bunker than a person of normal—that is, halfway brawny—stature, who'd tear his clothes and scrape his skin on the roughly plastered bunker walls.

And he leaped much more nimbly out of the cloud when the tippers full of ash were emptied outside on the dump. He'd stand off to the side with a pitying look, or rather a pitiless grin, while we sought cover under the tipper or waited with turned-up collars, bent backs braced against the exploding cloud, breathless, eyes closed, until the onslaught had passed. It was always blustery in the mine pits, and just as quickly as the ash flowed from the overturned tipper, it was beaten back as a scorching hot wave. Practice was required, and if you failed to anticipate the direction of the wind, you'd leap straight into an inferno meters high.

And finally, twice a month, Gunsch had to scribble something resembling his name in the proper column of the payroll when the secretary showed up in the boiler room with a little steel box full of money. — This, too, was one of the things that could just as well have been done by a deaf-mute.

I recalled a time I'd been able to observe the old man over the space of several days. It was a Christmas weekend, and then on past the New Year, when the holidays were canceled for Production Area 6 because of a special order. That of all times was when the temperature sank to minus ten Celsius; it was decided that a cold snap like that called for staffing the boiler room with two people, as the fifth boiler, regarded as the final reserve, had to be heated as well. No one wanted to work with Gunsch, and so I agreed to play the second man on his shift. — He doesn't talk much anyway, I thought, and besides, I probably have the fewest problems with his German.

I was quite mistaken; Gunsch talked the entire time, but only, it seemed, to himself. The old man muttered and snarled, he groused and griped without cease; from between the thin red lips, the only mobile part of his soot-smeared face, a relentless flood of words poured forth, now softer, now louder again and almost menacing. There was scarcely a word of German in it, and in moments of great difficulty I thought I caught the sort of Polish or Russian slurs I'd heard from my grandfather when he vented his rage at the world, the German-speaking world in particular.

After I'd spent half the shift ignoring them, his curses slowly but surely began to have an unpleasant effect on me. They weren't aimed at me, at least I couldn't imagine they were, but I was still part of the boiler room conditions which seemed to incur the old man's rage. I felt a long-familiar ferment begin within me. When we returned to the boiler room after our silent lunch break, and I instantly broke into a sweat in the scalding air over the boiler's iron cover plate, I noticed to my dismay that the old man was jabbering on.

Once and for all, would you shut up? I blurted out.

Gunsch paid no mind and cursed still louder, as though to drown out some sort of objections that barraged him from the past, from the filth and soot and barely breathable air of the present, or even from the future, which could never be anything but miserable. By chance, my gloved fist was clutching the red-hot iron hook used to open and shut the sliding doors to the boiler's feed chute; for a few seconds I was at the point of ramming the heavy thing into the old man's belly.

Shut up . . . just shut up! I bellowed. The old man faltered and stared at me with bloodshot eyes. Astonished, he didn't even seem to realize he'd been speaking. I saw that Gunsch dwelled in another reality; he was mad, constantly chattering with his ancestors or with ghosts of some kind . . .

For a long time after that C. was bothered by his fit of temper. It was one more thing that he'd probably inherited from his grandfather, or learned by watching him. And it was not without its hazards: there you go knocking out someone's teeth, or even knocking him dead, and then you've got to pay for it! No one will believe that you can't help this rage, that it's in your flesh and blood. And that this rage is made of memories that may not even be your own, premonitions or memories that were sunk within you without your really knowing them. Without your knowing it, a time bomb rests within you, ticking inside for years, for decades, and you never feel it. But someday it'll explode and kill an innocent person! thought C. And you're lucky if all you get is ten or twelve years in the slammer . . . and maybe you'll have to keep stoking in there, with a still older and lousier boiler, because those are your qualifications . . .

Among his most unpleasant memories were certain scenes that had transpired between him and his grandfather; he had never spoken of them. They always brought bouts of perspiration; the mere thought almost inevitably made him break into a sweat . . . when his grandfather worked up a sweat and his temper howled from within him, C. began sweating as well; in the blink of an eye he was speechless, choked by rage. Later, he told himself he'd merely wanted his grandfather's rage-twisted face to assume a different, pitiful expression, but that was an excuse. He'd grabbed the old man—in his eighty-year-old madness reduced to little but railing and ranting—by the throat, with fists long used to the crushing weight of iron and steel. Some lucky angel must have intervened, not a moment too soon; of their own accord his fists released the old man's neck.

When he thought about it, he was relieved that the old man was no longer alive; toward the end he'd persisted for days, indeed for weeks, in his rage, probably irked by nothing other than his own increasing infirmity. When it occurred to C. that the image of his grandfather's last years might presage his own future he was overwhelmed with dread. — Russian or Polish curses had always played a role in the altercations C. recalled. In these tongues, he felt, they sounded especially irate or even hate-filled. And then he'd seemed to hear them again from Gunsch's lips, and his temper, which he really felt was homicidal, had immediately flared up again.

In this host of curses there was one word that began with a guttural sound and escalated to a virtual eruption... almost a spewing of flame, thought C. — He recalled that it sounded like: *Holéra... holéra!* His grandfather had uttered it quite frequently, invariably during the most explosive rows in their tortuous family history; now it had shot from Gunsch's gorge in just the same way, lobbed into some random distance, though you couldn't tell for sure. It sounded malevolent; the word seemed to distill the sort of loathing that could mount only in the souls of eternally oppressed peoples or races. — C. had no idea what it meant, for he had always refused—and in this he resembled his mother—to learn even a few words of Polish or Russian. At some point he'd hit on the thought that it had to do with the name of a half-forgotten disease: *cholera*. And perhaps they used the word so often, my grandfather and Gunsch, because it resembled the German word *Kohle*, the term, that is, for the stuff at which they slaved each day, which filled their lungs with black deposits and forced black sweat from their pores. And then the ghastly name of the disease had become, for them, the quintessence of the clan that surrounded them: the clan was an insatiable plague sucking away their strength, wearing down their bones, transforming their hands into calloused paws that could never again be cleaned, drenching their gullets with tar and smoke so that nothing could free them up but floods of alcohol—and all that for the clan that ate them out of house and home . . .

When he was in town, visiting his mother, all these things came back to mind. That at least served to justify—at least in his own eyes—the visits of his, which had recently grown more frequent. When he returned to Berlin afterward, the tumult of the city slid like a screen in front of the thoughts from which he felt he was compounded. — What ought he to write about, if not *cholera* . . . he, C., who called himself a writer, albeit with a discomfort of which he seemed unable to rid himself? Ought he to write about Berlin, the city everyone else wrote about incessantly? Or should he write about his years navigating between East and West Germany, which had felt like a constant shifting back and forth between plague and cholera? He didn't know, and he refused to know. He'd come from cholera, and he seemed to have survived it, and perhaps he could write about that . . .

In Berlin, very rarely, he'd suddenly picture his mother, vegetating in the junk-stuffed, barely functioning flat he called a *slum*, to use a modern English expression for once. Growing older and older there, regularly falling asleep in the afternoon in front of the flickering, babbling television, as though no longer equal to the unwieldy mass of the consciousness hidden within her. And he knew that from the neighboring flats too, through the thin walls, the televisions could be heard: the breathless smarm of a host, the sycophantic applause of the audience, the perpetual, witless ooh-ooh of the mob, feigning enthusiasm over the sums of money or preposterous products flogged off on the never-abating game shows.

Amid that drivel she lay there on the red-brown couch, a thing that belonged on the junk heap, while in the yellow-tiled heating stove the spent coal crumbled to ash and cold seeped in through the crooked windows. She appeared to him then as a vessel of moldering memories that were undealt with, unspoken, that no one asked for, no one wanted to know about, and that began like unused coal to decompose.

Oh, how long these memories had led a life of their own, suicidal and shading into insanity. — What was left of the old woman, thought C., had long since been seized by a ferment of madness and little by little was being ravaged. — In some way, he thought, he was bound up with those memories that lay there swathed in thick, worn clothing, buried beneath woolen, coal-smelling blankets. — In some strange, barely explicable way, I am bound up with these memories, and no doubt I dread the moment in which they'll descend into utter confusion, flickering and vanishing into the void.

I only need to stumble on my way to the mailbox, and

already everything comes back to me. My foot only needs to catch on the uneven pavement, and at once I feel cast back into that time made up of never-ending winters. Of black winters covering other winters, black and long-decayed. And I ask myself over and over what I never asked myself then: What is it that lies beneath us? Bygone clans lie there beneath us. Long-forgotten clans lie down there, clans no one now asks about, clans long fermented to coal, clumped together blackly, clans rising up at night against the life that lives on above them. Rising up like the ferment of memories, like endless tribes of memories no one knows of now. And I am, yet again, the uncounted member of a clan surnamed *Choléra* that once set out early in the morning, at an inhuman hour, into the cold and the darkness that lay over the coal and over the ash. Ash lay over the coal, and coal lay over the ash. And my past lies down there, I thought, down beneath the coal, beneath the ash.

And I recalled one day when I'd tried to ask my colleague Gunsch about his background. One Sunday, the day after Christmas, the watchman had brought down a letter from the section head assigning me to the night shift in a different boiler room on Monday, December 27, because someone had called in sick. I didn't mind, it considerably shortened my way to work, but I immediately asked myself whether Gunsch had complained about my fit of rage two days before. I watched him as we worked and concluded that there was some dark thing in his obtuse skull that no light could be shed on. — No, he certainly hadn't complained, he had no interest whatsoever in demanding any rights. He might not even have been able to formulate a complaint; his capacity to express himself was so stunted that he no longer even understood what he was subjected to, short of pure physical pain. Moreover, he didn't even seem to believe in the necessity of disputing things. And when I thought about it, a similar reluctance or inability had arisen in me as well. — And so we're two creatures of the dark, used to keeping silent, I thought, and there are probably few things left in our minds whose expression would give another person any pleasure.

Perhaps it's that we're unable to love the world enough anymore. Why should we tell ourselves things about a world that matters less and less to us?

In other eras you'd set your memories before the world, convinced they'd find listeners or readers in coming times. But no one believes in coming times now, at least not here, in the class we belong to.

At the end of the shift, while we waited to be relieved, I did try to strike up a conversation with him. It was rather one-sided: Did you hear? Tomorrow I'll be sent off again to a different boiler room, tomorrow evening...

There was no sign that I'd been heard. The old man had returned from the showers and sat in the common room in his coat, wet hair plastered to his skull, audibly slurping the last of his coffee from his thermos cup.

Starting tomorrow you'll be on your own again, Gunsch! Too bad for you, it'll be quite a slog. But I have the feeling you don't care one bit...

He seemed to nod. Or did he merely sink his black watery gaze still deeper into the coffee cup, turning it in the black fingers of both hands?

Say, what neck of the woods are you from, Gunsch? My

grandfather was Polish too...we might even have been countrymen if certain things had happened differently. But then we'd probably just be shoveling coal in Poland or the Ukraine...

For a moment he showed a strip of pink gums with scattered yellow teeth in them; he seemed to grin. He'd jerked his thumb over his shoulder, toward the common room's coal-dust-smeared skylight; it seemed to me he'd mumbled a few words. If you followed the motion of his thumb, Gunsch had pointed across the mine pits, the direction indeterminate; perhaps he'd pointed in all directions, perhaps he'd described a circle whose trajectory lay in infinity. That afternoon the leaden hue of the sky merged on all sides with the vapors that rose from the freezing sheets of water at the bottoms of the mine pits; ever since morning an opaque atmosphere had ringed the whole horizon. When you came up the stairs from the boiler room, there was a smell of snow and glowing ash.

Maybe you don't have any family, Gunsch? No relatives...no relatives left? — I'd lost my confidence, my talk about "countrymen" seemed foolish; what nonsense, when speaking of regions that seemed to have no fixed borders. — I hadn't even been able to find my grandfather's hometown on the map. And it had never seemed to interest him which country he belonged to. When I thought of the mix of peoples in the chaos of regions Gunsch came from, of course he was no one's "countryman" in the strict sense. If you came from there, you were a leftover person, remembered by no one.

He grinned again and pointed his thumb at the floor, averting his eyes; there was a dull dog's look in them: They're all under the ground...

Those were perhaps the only words he'd ever really directed at me. And I asked myself whether I'd even understood him right. It didn't matter exactly what he'd said, at any rate he must have meant more or less what I had heard. — Walking back from the mailbox, it surprised me that I'd forgotten the words so quickly: *They're all under the ground...*

All at once I wondered if most people on this street weren't living with similar sentiments... Quite possibly that was the case! — Weren't they all, in some peculiar fashion, strangers? Of course they lived together, often harmoniously in their way, within their families they shared the quandaries and paltry pleasures of their existence, but they knew at all times how quickly they could lapse into oblivion... weren't they all forgotten the moment they stopped going to work? — They have a view of life focused on the bare present, thought C., on bare survival, on scraping by. — That's how they put it, you hear them say it often enough.

There was something disquieting in that: a feeling he only came to know once he'd already escaped from this existence. Ever since he'd begun to call himself a writer, he was gnawed by the suspicion that it was the lack of memories that thwarted him as a writer, that brought him to the verge of failure: the gaps in his memory, the incoherencies, the impossibility of reconciling spaces and times...

How many times he'd returned to the flat from his trip to the mailbox and first listened for a while at the door to the small back room where his mother slept. — Was she still breathing? — Dread filled him when he couldn't instantly hear her noisy struggle to breathe, when her restless tossing and turning on the mattress was not immediately detectable.

It was a noise as though the decrepit springs were slackening beneath the old woman's ever-lighter body and softly beginning to sing. — It's true, he thought, her body seems to be dwindling. And one day these fatigued springs of steel, these untuned strings, will cease to sing.

For a long while he sat in the kitchen with the door open and listened for noises from the back room. Sometimes it seemed, however hard he concentrated, that not another sound emerged. Muteness slipped under the door, flowed soundlessly down the narrow corridor, and began to spread like a cool breath of air in the kitchen. There, beyond the corridor, was a hermetic chamber filled with memories that pressed dumb and dark against the closed door; now speechlessness engulfed him even in the kitchen. And muteness reigned too on the floors below and above him; nowhere in this building, inhabited mainly by the aged, was there a sound, even on the street outside nothing more could be heard. He felt he could barely breathe now in this stillness, in the impalpable substance of the stillness. It was the hour when the town seemed utterly extinct ... always around the time when he jotted down a few inconsequential lines. On letter paper or a postcard: apologetic lines, sounding as though the writer's sole intent were to give just one more sign of life ... lines that would arrive in Berlin at some point, whose blue, shaky, dwindling script was the only proof that he existed. And that he then took to the mailbox, and sometimes this outlying part of town was so still that he feared his scurrying steps made too much noise. And then, almost aimlessly, he walked past the mailbox and on another hundred yards to the intersection beyond which the center of town lay.

It was as still as though the memory of his steps, of his stumbling, had been the last possible sound in this town. But soon, perhaps in another quarter-hour—you could already hear them from afar—it would be time for the first long-distance trucks to thunder from the left down the street that cut off his little neighborhood from the town proper. Now, at this still-nocturnal morning hour, the huge freight trains heading northward to Leipzig hurtled past the residential district at a reckless speed. Gusts of wind filled with ice shards and filth lashed into him. Though he stood on the sidewalk behind the guardrail, he felt a force that nearly made him reel back into the muddy grass behind him. When the deafening monsters passed through the town's periphery, they blew a warning with their horns; the long drawn-out howl, the blaring din of their passage, penetrated deep into the district to which, his hearing nearly obliterated, he now turned back.

He pictured his former colleague Gunsch again and wondered whether he wasn't under the ground as well by now. What a strange grin that was, over fifteen, maybe twenty years ago, at the end of the shift when he'd seen Gunsch for the last time. Hadn't that grin been like his grandfather's?... that grimace with a curse behind it: *choléra!* — He'd meant his clan; the coal; the darkness; he himself, a stranger to himself, ignorant of his forbears.

It began to snow again now, in late February or early March, as though winter were unable to have done with itself, and the wind blew stronger and stronger from in front. Once again C. felt on his face the icy breath he could not contend with; he saw light flare up behind a few windows in the houses, for just a few seconds, quickly extinguished.

The din of the long-distance traffic entered people's sleep and made them restless; like aimless ghosts they wandered their rooms, roused but not really awake, until they realized that it was still quiet on the street. But the traffic noise had come up against the wind, which seemed to turn stormy, so that C. had trouble making progress against it. And now it sounded as though imaginary thunderheads of din and ruin were surging through the sky above the roofs. Sometimes C. turned around to let the gusts spend themselves against his back... he thought of the waves of ash, blazing hot, that had descended on his bent back twenty years before. But no, on the street it was freezing cold!

He gazed up at the rows of buildings: perhaps it was true that most people who lived here belonged to a lost class. — That sounded histrionic, but wasn't it true that most of them had long since lost their work... and thus lived without their ordained purpose? Up there, behind the black windows in the ash-gray walls, dwelled the members of a refugee class among whom he had once counted himself.

Hardly any of them knew quite where they'd once come from, and no one pondered the question. And still less did they know where they were heading. And they didn't ask who would carry on the life and the work in which they'd had their share; that they had never asked. It had always been ordained by others. Those others derived this privilege from their ancestry... they'd inherited this ancestry and passed it on down; by ancestry they had the power to ordain how, where, and when the factories that exhausted the land would be built, maintained, and perpetuated: by those living behind the ash-gray walls of the buildings with the dark windows. For these people had no ancestry, they didn't think about their ancestry, they'd forgotten it, they'd forgotten their memories, their memories were all under the ground.

And though a forty-year-long attempt had been made to convince them that they themselves were to ordain the work in which they had their share, they hadn't understood it. Their purpose permitted no such understanding, for their purpose was so much older than they.

Perhaps it was as though an old dark deity governed them, a deity of the underground. It was a black god from endless past times who had altered them; he had altered their bodies and their minds, their hearts, their tongues, and their organs of procreation, he had altered the blood in their veins, in them it flowed a distinct touch more darkly and slowly, as though they all descended from that dark deity they no longer recalled . . .

They dwelled on above in the stifling air of their rental tombs, the damned who couldn't wake up after nights in which idleness kept them from sleeping. They had failed, they had little love for the world; when they gazed back, there were their fathers, their forefathers, but they were barely discernable—they had lived in the same shadow. The factories were closed, keys rusting in distant safes in Munich or Dortmund until they were sold to a demolition firm. If they were lucky, and not yet too old, they might find a job driving one of the long-distance freight trains transporting rolls of pink toilet paper or tins of condensed milk from Munich to Leipzig. — And looking ahead, they shuddered to think of their sons who went about with shaved heads, in combat boots and black bomber jackets, staring with alcohol in their eyes into a future that was none...

C. sat in the kitchen and listened to the wind, which made a soft, often polyphonic howling sound in the old building's flues. The fire in the heating stove had gone out; the cold could be felt, barely held back by ill-fitting windows. A murmur seemed to come from the neighboring apartments, the few of them with young people, cars started on the street, but the stillness of the kitchen went untouched. — Once, too, there were steps in the stairwell; they padded through his half-sleep, and he raised his head. He wondered if he'd heard the sound of the front door closing... just once, before the cars started up on the street; the sound was so familiar that he might easily have missed it. Or perhaps he'd only imagined the soft, shuffling steps in the stairwell. And then another door clicking into place, the door of the flat, just as familiar a sound. It seemed he hadn't fastened the safety chain to the doorframe, he'd forgotten...

And he'd left the door unlocked when he went to the mailbox. Afterward, he'd returned to the apartment with the absurd suspicion that someone had been there in the meantime. The smell of a stranger hung in the chilly air. There was quite clearly, almost too clearly, a muteness in the silence that was not his own muteness. Once again, for several minutes, he'd listened at the door of the little back room: not a sound had emerged. — Dark and bowed he stood holding his ear to the gray-yellow wood: in the room behind the door it was still.

What memories are sleeping, sleeping on behind that door... for how much longer? And after that I fell asleep at the table myself, deciding to postpone my trip to the mailbox until the next day, he thought. Or I only thought I did. And I only thought up the steps in the stairwell, they padded solely through my imagination. And then I thought I saw a shadow, dark and bowed, in the kitchen doorway, making a grotesque attempt to grin and saying:

They're all under the ground...

The words were hard to understand, like a noise I'd left far behind me, and they were swallowed by the stillness. Or drowned out by the town as it awoke at last.

THE DARK MAN

Best of all I seemed to remember the phone call with which the story began. The voice came from a pub, around ten in the evening, I heard the unmistakable background noises: a babble of voices, laughter, clinking glasses. I was not in the mood for a phone conversation; I was packing my suitcase with the TV on, and my relationship with my wife had reached rock bottom more than a week before. At first I thought it was a wrong number, I even hoped it was.

I'd like to see you, the voice declared, won't you come over? — It was a deep voice, if not exactly a bass, and might have been described as melodious had it not spoken so execrable a dialect, made still more distasteful by the evident effort to speak High German.

Where am I supposed to come ... and who wants to see me?

To the pub Zum Doktor, you must know the place. I'll be waiting for you at the bar.

Who wants to see me, is what I asked. And why, who am I dealing with here?

He didn't want to tell me on the telephone: Come on,

you'll find everything out soon enough, half an hour might even do the trick . . .

When I said nothing, he grew more insistent: I have to see you, it's imperative . . . come on, do me a favor!

But I don't have to do anything . . . what's the matter, anyway, what's this all about? — It struck me that he avoided the word "meet," using only the word "see"; I felt there was impatience in his voice, just a few shades away from a tone of command.

Can't you tell me what this is about already! If you don't tell me who I'm dealing with, what the matter is, I won't come!

That's a shame . . . that's a real shame! Nothing's the matter, I'd like us to have a few beers, it's on me.

I don't drink beer, I don't drink alcohol at all . . .

Oh! Then you've changed quite a bit, back then things were very different . . .

This was dragging on and on; at intervals we both fell stubbornly silent. — You won't tell me who you are . . . what this is about. — I sensed that all my questions were pointless.

If you have a beer with me here at the pub, I'll tell you.

Would I recognize you? I asked.

No, I should hope not. — Again he hesitated; by now I was shifting from foot to foot.

But it's sure to interest you, he went on, very much indeed. You are that writer, aren't you?

Don't act like you don't know exactly who you're dealing with. How about you tell me who I'm dealing with? . . .

You don't want to see me! he said, not sounding too disappointed, more contemptuous.

No, I can't, I don't have time. I'm flying to Dresden tomorrow morning, and I've got to get ready.

You really aren't coming?

No, goddammit...

Then I'm sorry to hear that, said the voice, a shade deeper. He didn't hang up at once, clearly waiting for me to change my mind. For half a minute I heard nothing but pub noise; the place must have been packed. He coughed into the phone—a heavy smoker—but didn't say a word. I heard him breathe laboriously, as though following physical exertion. I said nothing more either, finding the silence almost menacing. He cleared his throat, fastidiously, it seemed to me, and hung up.

Who was that? my wife asked. I was astonished; she hadn't said a word to me for days. Sitting in the kitchen behind the open door, she'd heard the entire thing.

Some crazy guy, I said. A nutcase who wanted to ask me to some pub. I don't know him...

Maybe you'll figure out who it was. Didn't you recognize his voice?

No, that's the thing, the voice didn't sound familiar at all. He was going to tell me who he was in the pub.

He definitely wasn't crazy, she said. He wasn't going to reveal himself except in public. Didn't that strike you? — That was an intelligent remark on her part; incidentally, I called her "my wife" only for simplicity's sake. We'd been living together for several years, for better and for worse, for some time now much worse, and thus far I'd refused to be chained down by marriage.

That evening it was taking me especially long to pack

my suitcase, and it was straining my nerves still more than usual—for fear of forgetting what I needed most, I regularly packed much too much unnecessary stuff—because I was constantly distracted by the inescapable jabber of the television, which had driven my wife into the kitchen. I felt a vague obligation to watch or hear what had been playing out on screen for more than an hour; it was one of those panel discussions—a so-called talk show—where people tirelessly, exhaustively, with exhausting repetitions and barely comprehensible fervor, debated a topic that for years, at least three years, I thought, had refused to go out of fashion: it was that the government had opened the archives of the defunct GDR's demised state security service. — How long the list had grown of the prominent figures, or self-appointed prominent figures, who were suddenly exposed as informers for that security service, or who, preempting the publicity, exposed themselves, which of course made them still more prominent. It was mostly authors who grappled with this subject or buried it under recurring torrents of verbiage; no one from the legions of the unknown, those whom, without the protection of fame, the Stasi had truly tormented, ever appeared on television. The writers talking on screen about the opening of several tons of Stasi files, talking it up and down—I knew several of them well, was even friends with them—seemed bent on making it the central theme of their literary lives... Ah! I thought, suddenly they have a real theme! — And they clung to this theme with such an iron grip, it was hard not to suspect that these files, suddenly made public, had saved their literary lives! And I wondered if they got fees for talking on television about Stasi files and Stasi informers... I didn't know, so far I hadn't taken part in any of these discussions... and I wondered whether the exposed Stasi informers who occasionally took part in the discussions received their fees as well. — No, they wasted not a word on what was happening with the earth, they didn't mention the depletion of the earth's ozone layer. Not a word on global climate change, the now-undeniable melting of the ice caps, the contamination of the atmosphere, the greenhouse effect that would inevitably bring undreamed-of catastrophes: their sole topic was the Stasi files... And no doubt they're perfectly justified, I thought.

I had applied for access to my own files as soon as I had grounds to suspect there were dossiers on me as well: so far my files had not been found. I registered that fact almost with relief, for the scant excerpts from other files I'd been shown—because my name cropped up in them—had exuded a boredom so paralyzing that I'd broken out in sweat. I literally feared these files—not that I'd learn they'd secretly made me out as an informer or a denunciator, something everyone who undertook to read their files had to reckon with, for the Stasi's mind worked in mysterious ways—I feared the gruel of language, these files' distinguishing feature, I feared the nausea, these paper monsters' brain-rotting stink, I feared the gray type, so like that of my own typewriter, I feared my face would break out in scabies if I submitted to reading these inhuman pages.

When at last I'd finished packing my bag and managed to turn off the TV—my wife had long since gone to bed—I sat at the table and smoked about five cigarettes in a row. My breath rattled, I panted as though I'd run a marathon or shoveled a ton of coal; I drank a whole bottle of mineral water and felt as though the greater part of the fluid immediately reemerged from my brow and my temples. And yet all I'd done was take a short walk, one of my routine walks up a narrow, steep street to a mailbox into which I dropped a hastily written postcard. — In the cool night air the whole situation had become quite clear to me: the mysterious call several hours ago and those endless panel discussions on the opening of the Stasi files— those two things were directly related.

A few hours later, early in the morning, as I started my trip—first in the taxi to the station, then in the various trains that brought me to the Frankfurt Airport—I had almost entirely suppressed the thought of that night's phone conversation. For several hours I'd tossed and turned, half asleep, getting up a few times to smoke, not daring to take a sleeping pill, which I would have had to steal from my wife, for fear of sleeping through the arrival of the taxi I'd ordered the day before. For some time my wife had refused to wake me when I had to get up early. — I'm not your mother! she hissed when I asked such things of her: I should finally learn to cope with the chaos of my life by myself. — My objection that she also lived from the money I earned with readings and events of that kind counted for nothing with her. Her voice lingered in my ear, asking from the bedroom on the upper floor if I'd been sure to mail all the letters to my bimbos, if I hadn't forgotten any; I'd made no reply. She had two rooms on the upper floor, a study and a bedroom; I had only one, on the ground floor, which served me both for working and sleeping . . . I paid the rent for this tiny house on the edge of town where the vineyards began, I paid the electric bills, I covered the rising costs of the heating oil we used in winter, but I hadn't the slightest interest in confronting her with these things; I had my back to the wall and said not a word, I'd had as much as I could take of our constant quarrels. But my silence wounded her all the more; she took it as an affront... I was hurt by her silence as well, but eventually felt almost grateful I didn't have to hear her voice, in which I seemed to hear nothing but aggression. I no longer touched my wife, I avoided her, I shut myself in my study, filled with dense cigarette smoke, where late at night or early in the morning I tried to fall asleep amid coughing fits and nausea. And my coughing fits would disturb my wife's sleep, and there'd be new grounds for a quarrel. In fact I did correspond irregularly with several "bimbos," as my wife put it; when I was away she searched my desk, and naturally found stowed in the drawers the letters I'd received from the "bimbos," and systemati- cally spotted the erotic or sexual components—how to put it?—which the letters contained; she spotted them even in the phrases where they weren't. Of course my wife wasn't entirely in the wrong; a long time ago I'd brought back a stack of postcards from Holland that, if you really wanted to, you could describe as pornographic. When my wife noticed the stack of these postcards growing smaller and smaller, she told me to my face that she understood perfectly what kind of correspondence I was conducting; and she called this correspondence nothing less than "swinish." I couldn't even shake my head at that.

There was one case, though, for which my wife made an exception: Marie, who lived in Leipzig. I had known her a good deal longer than my wife, and with Marie I really had

had a short-lived love affair. When it came to Marie my wife held off, Marie never came up in the tangled mass of her reproaches; evidently, in the manner of feline predators, she granted her a certain prior claim, or it was simply that, in Marie's case, I'd been honest to my wife for once and told her about it. — I'd never told her a thing about the other so-called affairs: in those there had never been any opportunity for physical contact, nothing of the kind, and that was probably why I was ashamed; it was the shame of failure, and my wife, however mistakenly, managed to goad it within me again and again. — I noticed that now and then she talked to Marie herself: the last time was just a few days ago; and then my wife had handed me the receiver and indicated that Marie wanted to talk to me.

I was alarmed by the voice that emerged, a mere wisp, from the telephone. Marie said she wasn't well, no, not at all, kept alive by a constant haze of morphine, but it would all be over soon now. The end was near, that she knew, it would only be a matter of days or weeks. — Marie's voice barely breathed into my ear, as absent as though it came from another universe; the long pauses between words were filled with labored breaths that seemed deafening after her voice. — Following her last cancer operation, just as unsuccessful as all the previous ones, she was lying, her body slit, in her tiny room in Leipzig, dependent on the care of a friend, a painter who'd come to stay a few days ago, though the apartment barely fit two people. — You've got to see her one more time, my wife said after I hung up. If she's even still there, you can be sure it's the last time you'll see her. And you've planned enough time on your crazy trip to Dresden and your mother...

For flying to Dresden, my wife had declared me certifiably insane. A new academy had been founded there—in the East new academies were springing up like mushrooms—and I had been invited, along with several other poets, to read fifteen minutes of poetry at the inaugural event. The reading fee was negligible; besides, I'd booked a flight, albeit one of the cheap flights you could get if you reserved in time, and the trip included a weekend. The academy could only reimburse train trips, and so I had wound up with a losing proposition that vexed me quite enough without my wife's derision. — She told me I was acting like a whore. All they had to do was wave, and there I was. — Whores generally get paid pretty well, I retorted. — True, she said. But not the old, beat-up whores.

After that quarrel we gave each other the silent treatment for more than a week. In secret I had to admit she was right; just to save some time for a certain piece I wanted to work on—which, I persuaded myself, I could best do at my mother's . . . because the manuscript was set in the town south of Leipzig where I was born and where my mother lived on in the same apartment, now almost utterly dilapidated—just for that I had dreamed up this idiotic itinerary: the best part was that I was planning to jettison the return flight from Dresden, since the train from Leipzig to Frankfurt am Main was actually quicker. — But now I'd lose the time I had gained: on the postcard I'd taken to the mailbox the night before my departure, I'd told Marie I planned to visit her in Leipzig . . . just for a few hours, a single afternoon, due to time constraints, but I hoped, or so I'd written, that she'd look forward to seeing me again. — If I spent days hanging around at my mother's first, my wife had declared, it might be too late to visit Marie...

Maybe, the thought crossed my mind, before taking the train back from Leipzig I could pay Marie a second visit... a farewell visit! I thought.

Nervous and bleary-eyed, I sat on the suburban train to Mannheim, where I had to change for the so-called airport shuttle to Frankfurt Airport, and kept running through the stops of my trip in my mind. I was passing through the vast wine-growing region that lay below the Palatinate Forest: vineyards, nothing but vineyards, and the sun rising over them. I was traveling through a landscape of pure cultivation; it was, in my view, one of the most beautiful regions in Germany, and so far it had not appeared in a single work I'd written. Though I'd lived here for several years, I wrote on and on about the moonscapes south of Leipzig, stretching to the horizon, on and on about the industrial town of my birth, surrounded by pits from whose fathomless depths lignite had once been mined. Now there was nothing but dead, shut-down mine pits, and those tracts of land seemed to have lapsed into an irreversible futility, a uselessness that dragged each of my thoughts into the depths to shut it down and make it useless. — Or I wrote on and on about journeys, confused and haphazard, more like evasive actions, flights without cause, without aim, a perpetual flight in the wake of a crime committed only in a dream...

Here, all the way to the horizon, across the whole Rhine Plain, the stuff of human pleasure was coaxed forth from the earth, here there was nothing but vineyards. And when it grew light and a beautiful day dawned, hosts of birds swooped down into the vines, whose grapes were nearly ready for the harvest. And at the edges of the plots, sometimes still lapped by mist, the field wardens came to life, appearing out of nowhere and firing their shotguns wildly into the air to scare off the raucous flocks of birds.

Before reaching Dresden—that city so ravaged during the war, then ravaged once again by the so-called reconstruction the GDR had indulged in... and now perhaps for the third time, I thought, by the mass of exhaust fumes that found no escape from the Elbe valley where Saxony's new capital nestled—and two days later, on the express train from Dresden to Leipzig, I had plenty of time to think. Again and again the newspaper slipped from my fingers as I tried to read, my head fell back against my seat in the compartment where I was the sole passenger, and the twilight of half-sleep engulfed me, more restful, I found, than the mindless non-place deep sleep plunged me into when, rarely enough, I achieved it. You could sleep and yet you could think, quite lucidly even—a surprisingly satisfactory state! Oddly, I thought less about what might await me in Leipzig; I couldn't get my mother out of my head, who over the years had grown very quiet and old, meekly fulfilling my every wish... and for my wife this very meekness constituted an offense whose magnitude unsettled me, for increasingly she traced my behavior—my lack of character!—back to my mother's. There were no such frictions in my mother's home: when I needed peace and quiet, I was left in peace; Mother asked me no questions and expected none from me; she let me sit alone in the kitchen, bent over some draft; she made herself invisible in the next room and even turned off the television if it bothered me... and she'd make me more tea when she saw that the pot on the kitchen table was empty.

It occurred to me to simply stay with my mother as long as I wanted, to work there on my manuscript as long as I wanted. My mother had no telephone, my wife couldn't reach me... the idea of vanishing from her horizon for a while, leaving her in the dark, suddenly filled me with the calm that made me nod off in the train. I knew it was a lust for revenge, however modest... but at least it was the opposite of the panic I fell into whenever my wife threatened to throw me out or go her own way.

Excruciating tensions had arisen nearly every time my wife and mother met... which could happen only in our house in Rhineland-Palatinate, for my wife refused to travel to the east. It was, admittedly, my wife's house; she had found it, leased it, and furnished it as she saw fit, for here, I had to admit as well, I had proven completely incompetent... and it remained my wife's house, even if I paid the rent each month. Every time my mother visited us, which she did once or twice a year for little more than a week, the same thing happened: my wife felt ousted from her house, seeking refuge in a village with one of her girlfriends, where, I could feel it in the air, she waited as though on a bed of nails. During this time my mother was charged with watering the countless plants that stood about everywhere, a task my wife wouldn't entrust me with, regarding me as completely unreliable... and my mother overlooked a ten-inch-high orange tree that stood all by itself in a clay pot on a windowsill: the tree had dried up and couldn't be revived... it was my wife's favorite plant. From that point onward, open hatred erupted; the next day I tried to persuade my mother to leave because we were busy and had no more time for her. My wife refused to drive Mother to the train station in her car; I called a taxi and took her to the little station, which would have been a good forty-five-minute walk with an old woman like Mother. I stood mute, close to tears, on the platform next to my mother, who had no idea what had just spun out of control.

What had spun out of control was my wife's rage; she regarded us both, my mother and me, as people who were devoid of independence, eternally anxious to do everything right, and who for that very reason—because they were constantly trying to hide, to avoid reproaches…because they had no desires and no questions…because they skulked about the house as though under some tyranny from which a devastating verdict might come at any moment—for that very reason did every possible thing wrong. — You people show no initiative, my wife said, all you've learned is how to wait for orders, you have no sense of self, and that's why you can't enjoy life in this little house of mine…

One time, I defended myself and accused my wife of acting like a Permanent Mission of the Federal Republic of Germany. When we were on her territory, we had damn well better be happy and show it. If we didn't, we were an unacceptable proposition for the country that had just annexed its brothers and sisters from the other side. — You let yourselves be annexed with the greatest of pleasure, she said, things couldn't move quickly enough for you. But lead independent lives—that you can't do! — And she added that Marie was the only person she knew who'd at least tried to live independently…

My wife was not entirely wrong. But she was unaware that Marie had lived *too* independently, that ever since the reunification we were constantly discussing she'd been unable to find her way to the welfare office, that she avoided going to the doctor because she was uninsured. And that was probably why her cancer had been diagnosed far too late. Marie lived more or less from handouts, but no one was allowed to mention it. I, too, had occasionally slipped a hundred-mark note into the purse that hung from her doorframe, secretly, knowing it would have humiliated her...

Over time my messages to Marie, sent on postcards, had grown sparser, arid, monosyllabic; it struck me that she virtually never replied to my mail. She gave no more response than to the bills I slipped her. When I had a chance to phone I'd ask if she'd received my letters or cards... and she would ask in return which letters and cards I meant. She probably would have responded the same way to a question I didn't ask: Which hundred-mark bills do you mean? — This behavior was typical of Marie: if you sent something her way, she simply didn't seem to notice. And she seemed not to notice when someone desired her; if you ended up in bed with her, she merely seemed to follow some sort of imaginary instructions... though I put this down to my inability to show my desire, much less articulate it, which I felt was one of my innermost weaknesses...

Filled with thoughts of this kind, I arrived in Leipzig: I saw at once that it was too late for all my questions. Marie's bed had been moved into the tiny kitchen, close to the gas stove, as though now, in mid-September, heat was already needed... often, as I recalled, Marie had heated with the flames of the oven, because coal was too expensive. And often enough I'd told her it was dangerous. By the bed stood a narrow table with the telephone, dirty dishes, and a quantity of open vials containing various morphine preparations. Next to them, in a torn-open envelope, I saw the card I'd written her a few days before. — It had arrived that morning, Marie said. — The painter who had let me in, a girlish creature with short blond hair, sat sketching in the next room, keeping an eye on things in the kitchen through the open door. Marie lay in bed in a white nightgown, speaking in a voice as soft as a breath, barely a whisper now, the words slipping, incorporeal, from lips that barely moved. Between words she caught her breath, smiling as though to apologize for the long pauses. — Could she show me her stomach, she asked; gingerly she pushed aside the blanket and lifted up her nightgown. Her abdomen was crisscrossed by bluish-red, barely-healed scars. Next to the alarmingly thin body a plastic bag collected her urine drop by drop.

Later, on the bus on the way to my mother, I remembered glimpsing for a few moments, barely covered by the white nightgown, her breasts, which alone were still completely unscathed. Marie seemed to know full well that I was staring much less at her wounds than at those breasts, those still-smooth, soft hemispheres, bared halfway up the brownish nipples . . . those breasts were still firm and their beauty was flawless. Smiling, eyes alert, she had acknowledged my gaze; there was irony in her eyes as she pushed the nightgown down again. I knew this irony; it had been in her gaze whenever I said goodbye to her, when, late at night, I went out her door and she shut it softly behind me.

Why hadn't I given in to impulse and laid my hands on her breasts? As ever, the target of Marie's irony had been my suppressed desire . . . as ever, when I left late at night, irked that I couldn't make up my mind to spend the whole night with her . . .

But perhaps, I thought, there would be another chance to visit . . .

Around eight in the evening, in a turmoil, I arrived at my mother's; she seemed pleasantly surprised. — I almost wasn't home, she said. You know I often go to the theater on Fridays. But today they're showing something I've seen twice before. — You know I've still got a key, I said. And I always have it with me when I come without telling you. — That's right, she said, I almost forgot that . . . did you write me that you were coming? — I don't think so. — My mother forgot many things, now that she was going on eighty. What she never lost was her gentleness and solicitude toward her son, having forgotten all the old rancor over my unreliability, and especially my frequent drinking. — I ate almost nothing that evening, wouldn't let my mother make me tea, making it myself instead; I'd already put my notebooks on the kitchen table, a sign that I wasn't up for conversation . . . several years ago my mother had begun taking my writing seriously, and accepted my silence. — I immediately began another card to Marie, telling her I meant to visit again on Monday, because, as I said, I'd been annoyed with myself for not staying a little longer today. Or not spending the whole night with her. — When she read the card on Monday, I knew, she'd have that ironic smile in her eyes again. — However—I added this qualifier at the end of the card—she shouldn't hold it against me if I didn't come, because I had to catch my flight from Dresden to Frankfurt early Monday evening, and I might have trouble making the connections. — On Monday, yes, if Marie was to have the card on Monday, I had to put it in the mailbox that night, at any rate by nine the next morning. It was always the same thing with me, the last act of my day's twenty-four hours before I tried to find sleep was a five-hundred-meter trip to the mailbox.

After Mother had gone, I sat in the kitchen, thinking back on the afternoon. Outside, salutary darkness shrouded the small industrial town, which, following the so-called *change*, had swiftly metamorphosed into a sociopolitical rubble heap of vacant houses, empty shops with dusty windows, and defunct factories. The town didn't even have a policeman now; that was perhaps the clearest benefit of the change so far. But a benefit for whom? If there was a chicken thief on the loose, you'd have to phone the riot squad in the district capital, a difficult matter, there being no phone booths here.

The sad jokes that came to my mind: I thought back on my life, on afternoons, countless overlong afternoons I'd draw out into the first light of dawn . . . indeed, my life, what I called *my life*, had unfolded in the afternoons, in idle afternoons—and a few of them I had spent with Marie. I had always gone again in the evening, at least at a time when I could catch the last train from Leipzig.

That afternoon in Leipzig, as I sat on the edge of her bed, I had sensed that this thin body was now subject to doubt, already in the process of dissipating. More and more it seemed to take on the color of the bedclothes, barely standing out against them. I had tried to encompass this body with my gaze, as though compelled to imprint it on my brain ... How much longer would it be possible to *see* her? — Below her navel, where the surgical scars made a star shape on her skin, a small wispy patch of light appeared, seeming to circle the wounds, atremble; the afternoon sun cast it through the ground floor window across from her bed. In the next room too, the bedroom where the painter now lived, these flecks of light had often come in the late afternoons. When the sun sank toward the west, its rays broke here and there through the tall dense yew hedge that bordered the yard outside the windows, and for a brief time aimed their vibrating spears at the glass and the curtains. — When this light disappears, so I'd thought, then I'll go ...

I gazed at her slender white thighs, which were seized now and then by an infinitesimal tremor; Marie said no more, breathing heavily. Her legs were shut, and I saw the small flat pubis, whose hair had always been light and transparent; now it was denuded. — Why hadn't I gotten up, shut the door before the painter's eyes, and lain down beside the white body whose contours slowly slipped into nothingness? — There was some incomprehensible darkness inside that had stopped me, and to the end of my life it would fill me with profound regret.

Here too the trip to the mailbox took little more than five minutes if I walked quickly. It led toward the town center, ultimately just an extension of the main street that cut across town from east to west. We had always lived on this street; behind us, a few hundred yards on, the town expired, petering out into the allotment gardens on one side and the ranks and echelons of garages and the premises of small service companies on the other; then the street broke off, splitting into a delta and sinking away into the mud and the stillness. A short way further rose the wooded hills climbed by winding, stepped paths. But you could no longer enter the forest: it had been bought up by the architectural offenders who were erecting their single-family homes behind tall chain-link fences or stockades, Tyrolean or Upper Bavarian travesties with stag's antlers over the brown-stained wooden balconies . . . built with the money they'd made at the ramshackle kiosks that filled every empty lot in town, where the jobless fed on fatty, evil-smelling West German bratwurst and cans of beer from Dortmund and Bremen. With the authorities' blessing they sawed up the forest and covered it with concrete, and in the vestiges left standing they drilled their attack dogs. — It was the forest of my childhood, and it loomed behind me when I walked to the mailbox, and in the warm time of year on my way back from the mailbox I saw the sky grow light over the last stands of trees. And more and more often in recent years I felt depression shadow me as I returned.

The mailbox is mounted on the front of the so-called "main co-op," as many of the town's inhabitants still refer to the building complex. Once it was the largest of the town's stores; today it has become a rather pitiful chain supermarket with small crammed shelves. The upper floor—the former clothing, stationary, tool, and toy departments, and on the other side facing the courtyard, the administrative office for all the cooperative stores in town and the surrounding area—is vacant, apparently impossible to lease out. Behind the sales building . . . in the fifties, before there were self-service shops,

Mother had manned the cash register, whose drawer opened with a jingle at the turn of a crank, surrounded by several sales clerks who served the customers under her supervision... on a side street, beside the entrance to the multistory administrative wing... whose endless wooden stairs I had to climb to pick up a form to attend the co-op's children's camp on the Baltic... across a granite-cobbled yard looms the hulk of the former industrial bakery, its courtyard surrounded by nineteenth-century façades of dark-red brick, with stone steps outside and ramps with guardrails where the delivery trucks used to line up and load the bread... so that the whole side street smelled of it, freshly baked, still warm... and drove off, fully laden, through a massive cast-iron gate: from here the town, the surrounding villages, and the industrial plants were supplied with this chestnut brown, eternally same-tasting foodstuff—a kilo for fifty-two pfennigs... the bread was of incomparable quality, and it never changed. Now the bakery is empty too, cleared out, abandoned to decay.

Pardon me, could you give me a light?

It is this hackneyed code phrase that startles me from my sentimental thoughts, far too trite to convey to me what it stands for: imminent danger!

I give him his light, and the lighter, which I have to click several times, illuminates his face; a face between fifty and sixty, the age at which you try once again to lose weight, because the mellowing effect fat has on the face is gradually wearing off. But you won't look striking again, merely wrinkled, and a stubbly beard, generally gray-white, heightens the impression of something aimless and unformed. Little gray eyes, eternally on the lookout: Don't worry, we're alone, no one will disturb us ... I'd rather I could hide in a throng of people—a crowded pub, for instance—all at once the square seems bleak and much too large: like a square in a dream whose edge, however fast you walk, you'll never reach in time, and may never reach again. Dawn is breaking, it grows brighter and brighter; that too is repugnant.

You'll have guessed right off who you're dealing with, eh?

I say nothing at all; off the phone he's still speaking that High German he'll never really learn. But he no longer speaks it with such fastidious reserve; there's an oafish familiarity in his injections of dialect. — What does this bastard want from me, with his bad conscience written all over him? I think. Of course I know this can take a different turn quite quickly; I'm curious how he'll start chipping away at my conscience, they learned that at their so-called *Firm*.

How long will you be staying? he asks me amiably. Getting away from it all for a few days, eh? Visiting the old homeland again ...

Old homeland, that's reactionary language! That's the sort of thing you always accused the radical Bonn imperialists of, I say.

Oh! Do you suppose I ever dealt with that—language usage? What do you think we were doing the whole time? We didn't have time to kill with language usage. Although ... sometimes I'd rather have had that to deal with. You'd be surprised how much alike we would have been.

Us ... alike, okay! Why don't you explain to what I owe this honor. I know, back then you didn't have to, but times have changed. Fortunately for me, unfortunately for you!

True, times have changed . . . He opens his eyes wide as though he's only just realized it . . . What do I want? Well, nothing, there's nothing I can want anymore. But I'd like to take a stroll around the block with you and tell you something. Something about myself, if you're interested. — He lights a new cigarette from the glowing butt; a heavy smoker, as I'd suspected.

I don't want to hear it, I say. I'm not some Father Confessor. Let's go our separate ways, I don't know you and you don't know me. You've done nothing to me, probably not, and I'll do nothing to you.

You don't know I've done nothing to you, he says.

Come on, let's drop the whole thing. As you see, I'm the more successful of us two, I've got academies falling all over themselves. Now you just let me do my thing in peace, I'm not going to give you any absolution. And certainly not a job reference.

Maybe you got a reference like that from me one time, you just don't know it. Could be, eh? — I see him grin in the morning light. — But this isn't getting us anywhere. Come on, join me for a bit!

He noticed I hadn't given him a clear enough dismissal, but that probably wouldn't even be possible. The clearest *no* bounces right off them; if there's anything they've learned, it's how to ignore rejection. I light a cigarette as well:

All right then, let's walk around the block . . .

I wasn't one of those who had to loiter on the street, he begins his story. At least not for long, I didn't do so well there. Pretty soon I stumbled up the ladder, they saw what I was better at, and soon I had a desk job. I liked dealing with written material, but I wasn't terribly good at writing reports. I handled evaluations: for instance, this and that is perfectly fine, this or that can go through, or that there mustn't get where it's going. In other words, I read the things my poor victims wrote, and believe it or not, I always served them well...

That's what they all say!

I know, but still, that's how it was. If there was something in there that was outright embarrassing, I kept my mouth shut. Tighter shut than the people who'd written these things... He laughs and chokes on his smoker's cough.

You're trying to tell me that the... the victims had no idea what a friend you were to them?

Oh! He's still coughing. That's nice of you, but honestly, it's much too nice...

So, if you weren't a stool pigeon on the street, what were you, a kind of case officer?

I don't know exactly, and it doesn't matter anyway. We called ourselves a secret service, you know, so we were secret on every level. As I said, I stumbled up the career ladder quite quickly. If I'd wanted to, I could have asked to get an informer...a stool pigeon, we called them that ourselves. And I tried two of them, but they didn't pan out. You'll... you'll laugh, but I'd have liked to get you...

Very flattering, I say. What was so appealing about me?

Oh, he says, you were difficult, that's all. You were unreliable, always caught up in your own craziness. And that would have been totally convincing. You were always running away from things, completely egotistical, phony, and neurotic, a real artist, in other words. All that stealthiness of theirs was second nature to you, they wouldn't have had to give you a new image. Officers with charisma, no, we had enough of those. But you . . . you would have been *it*!

Well, and . . . what put you on to me, anyway?

Quite simple, I was responsible for reading the mail.

You'll excuse me for thinking that's a pretty sleazy job. Quite clever, by the way, to wait for me here at the mailbox.

Yeah, that was kind of dumb! He says it with a grin. But we always did call for an ability to free-associate. Besides, you didn't want to go to the pub with me. And incidentally, sometimes I'd wait for you at the mailbox back then, too; there was a vacant apartment nearby, and I could watch when you came, almost always at the same time. But I did that on an extracurricular basis, it was almost a hobby of mine. As I said, I started to take quite an interest in you.

A hobby! I repeat. So that's why you're here . . . you're just keeping up your hobby!

Sensing the anger in my voice, he suppresses his ironic tone effortlessly:

It was more than a hobby! I can tell you—in this case I was more on your side than on my Firm's. It's true, you were an extracurricular pursuit of mine, even after closing shop, so to speak.

But that's how your Firm wanted it. Vigilance by day and night, round the clock, isn't that so?

You know your stuff, he noted dryly, but you misunderstood me. I meant the big closing-shop . . . I meant when everything closed down, the state, the Party, us, the party newspaper, and the whole centralism thing. Don't you think we still had a few people in the post offices afterward who

were quite capable of picking out the things we needed...?
Oh, give me a light again, would you!

I give us both a light, and we go on walking our common
path; I'm silent while he speaks:

You know, your private letters interested me more than
your, so to speak, business correspondence. Hey, don't get
excited, now...by the way, I know that for you everything
was private. Even your business dealings with publishers and
so on, that was ultimately private as well. That was the thing
about you...

You call those business dealings!

Well, that was how you made your living...sometimes
better than I, but that's not what it was about for me, that
you can believe. I was more interested in the human side, as
they call it. Now you'll yell that we had to be interested in
that side, working for the Firm...oh yes, I know all that. Let
me tell you, more than once I risked a disciplinary transfer
for failing to report certain things, practically hushing them
up...

Heroic! A resistance fighter, that's what you were!

Just as little as you. As heroic as you. When I read your
mail, sometimes I'd sit there thinking, what business is this of
mine? Here I am, I thought, constantly dealing with all this
paperwork, and what am I missing out on in the meantime?
Nothing the whole time but letters, letters, words, phrases!
And now and then you take notes, and they're in writing
too. It's like a blanket of writing covering everything...and
often enough it's illegible writing! A film you maybe can't
see through anymore. A haze of writing...and can you
even still see the life behind it? Is there actually still flesh

behind the writing? Or just more writing? Does this writing mean just writing now, or did there use to be something else behind it? Is this writing just writing about itself... didn't there use to be women there somewhere? But is a woman really still what this guy means? These were the things I thought about.

A haze of writing, I repeat, that's probably quite well put.

It could've come from you. Maybe it really did come from you, and I just... what's the literary term... appropriated it?

You read it somewhere. Still, I don't doubt that you really felt these things.

Yes, well, I was a real bloodhound. I even found out the woman you were writing those lovely cards and letters to. I don't know if you remember her, it's ten years ago now. Ten years ago or longer, first the cards came from the east, then suddenly from the west. I mean that little woman from Leipzig, who wanted to be a writer too... nothing like you, of course! Marie A. was her name, I think, just like in Brecht. A name for a Madonna, eh...?

He breaks off; with his keen instincts he noticed quite well how I flinched. I'd flung the half-smoked cigarette in the gutter and immediately lit another one. The name's been said... I feel I've been expecting it the whole time. I don't know how to describe my feeling: rage or horror; at any rate, I feel exposed... a feeling they still manage to provoke, with the same ease as ten years ago.

Ah, you're seeing red, he says. Take it easy, we're men of the world, after all!

Her name was Marie H., not Marie A., I say. But I'd rather we stayed on the subject of literature. You know the poem by Brecht... could you explain that to me, so I can be impressed?

No, no! he replies with a laugh; it seems to hold something like relief. No, it's nothing, really...

I say nothing, taking hasty drags from my cigarette; without my noticing, we've already passed the mailbox and are heading around the block for the second time. — He's got a hold on me, I think, just the way he meant to! With an effort I remind myself that I must have an edge on him as far as my relationship with Marie goes; he can't know how things stand *now*; he's speaking of a state that's passed, washing the dirty linen of his memory... all the same, it's a nightmare.

I don't have to let you shock me anymore, I mumble, not anymore, you're harmless!

Oh, that Brecht poem, he says. The little cloud! You see, we do have more in common than you'd think.

Had, I say, we *had* more in common! Enemies always have something they share, that's a truism. But we have nothing in common now.

You weren't my enemy, he says with that grin on his mug again. When he sticks in the next cigarette, I'll hold up the lighter flame to his filthy three-day beard, and when he staggers back, I'll beat him to the ground.

No, you weren't my enemy, he repeats; he's observing me now, walking a stride behind me, and I wait for him with my head turned to the side, on my guard. He speaks as though under some kind of pressure:

I was forced into it, simply forced by the situation, I had nothing at all against you personally. I know, they all say that these days, and it's not something you need to hear. I just want to confess that sometimes all I wanted was to erase your signature from the cards you wrote Marie A. and add my own there instead... My little cloud! Didn't you write her that?

Hardly, I say, that's a figment of your imagination! But did you do it, did you add your signature? Whatever happened to the cards you read, anyway?

Of course I didn't do it, and it would have been tough anyway, since you wrote in ink... though we had ways of dealing with that too. But it would have been too risky, with people breathing down my neck. What happened to them? They were read and passed on, as a rule.

Passed on where? And what wasn't the rule?

If there was nothing relevant in them, they continued on the normal postal route, quite simple. Of course, copies would sometimes be made of certain things, but that wasn't the rule with you.

And you can't recall there ever being something relevant?

Not that I know of. Unlike you, I can remember quite well. I was the only one who was personally interested in you... that was what I lacked, you see, a little cloud like that.

Could you stop with that goddamned cloud already! She wasn't a cloud for me... and she still isn't. Another thing, can you remember making copies of my letters too?

Goodness me, I couldn't do that, we kept scrupulous lists of every copy we had to make. But you're probably asking because you're still fond of her? Or you're actually involved with her—I always wished that for you. Though I envied you. I even went to see Marie A., made a special trip out to her part of Leipzig, trespassed on someone else's beat, and questions were asked, very embarrassing questions. And then I envied you all the more . . . how can I manage to write little A. those kinds of letters and postcards, with such lovely photos from Amsterdam? I pored over those cards of yours. But building on what was in the postcards, I would have started expressing myself more clearly, I wouldn't have left it all in this lovely haze. For me, she wouldn't have stayed a cloud, or a Madonna up there in the clouds . . .

And after a while he said: I wonder if it's this haze that's still so appealing to you. Times have changed, no one has to read between the lines anymore. You don't need to be left out in the cold, as you once put it so nicely. Did you just make that up too? No, you don't need to do that anymore, you're successful enough now, now you can reach out and take what you like . . . and I've helped out a little there, I'll have you know.

What did you help out with?

That doesn't matter; I don't want to brag in front of you. You . . . you can go looking for life now, after all it does exist . . .

Behind the haze of words! I say, leaning exhausted against the mailbox, where we've arrived again. I've had enough, I'm not looking for life now, I'm looking for an escape. I won't come along for a third time.

I've talked myself blue in the face, haven't I? Shall we have one last smoke? Don't tell me it wasn't interesting for you!

We light up again; it's my last cigarette, and I put the empty pack in my pocket, there being no wastebasket nearby. — Interesting or not, I still don't understand what you actually want, I say. Surely we have less in common than you think. By the way, I'm sure there were other men who were interested in Marie A., and who . . .

Oh! he shakes his head. Don't speak ill of her, no one has that right. I'll always defend her!

Where she is now, she can do without your defense, believe me.

Sure, he says, I'll have to take your word for that. But one more thing . . . I've got to finally come out with it, the reason I had to see you. I've still got one long letter and a few of the cards you wrote her. I wanted to give them to you.

I was barely surprised, as I recall. — Come on, I snarled, hand them over, they're my letters! What took you so long?

I wanted to get an idea of you first . . .

And is the idea such that you can finally give me the letters? How many do you have, anyway?

Quite a nice big stack. But I don't have them here, I didn't know for sure if I would see you. I can't go carrying everything around with me all the time. Where I'm living now, one of my superiors might crop up, you never even know them all yourself. I hid the stuff . . . I'll bring it tomorrow. Same time tomorrow, right here, and we'll take another stroll around the block, eh?

I returned to the flat in indescribable agitation. — Could I believe what I'd just been through, or had it been a figment of my imagination? I'd turned around when I was halfway home: he'd already vanished; I hadn't seen the direction he'd gone off in. Or had he not been there in the first place . . . had I gone mad? In this town there was a person who knew more about me than I about him . . . which might not be unusual.

The only unusual thing was the way in which he had acquired his knowledge: it was almost as though he'd appropriated my life, or at least a part of it, a part—I suddenly knew—which had meant a great deal to me.

I tried to remember how he looked, his face, his build... and strangely, as I did so, I looked into the mirror, as though I could remember his face only with the help of my own. — Why hadn't I taken at least one good look at him? He had *seen* me, but I hadn't seen him...

His face... I thought. It was unshaven, I was unshaven too; the nicotine of many cigarettes had left a yellow-brown rim in the stubble on his upper lip; on my upper lip I saw the same yellow-brown shadow. He was about my size and stature; he wore a jumpsuit of dark, glossy material, dark-blue or black: a jogging suit, that was what they called it these days... it was the uniform of the early retirees and the jobless who loitered at the kiosk hour after hour with their canned beer... It was a catastrophe: the collapse of the system had even robbed people's resolve to dress themselves at their own discretion.

I felt there had been many more similarities between us... when I thought of my wife, the image she had of me— and never wearied of confronting me with—perhaps it was really an image of him. His character, I thought, had that mixture of self-loathing and calculation that employs truth and lies indiscriminately... for years my wife had offered therapy for a comparable sickness in me. My hopeless submission to every authority—or everything I regarded as an authority—had enmeshed me in an inextricable snarl of half-truths, evasions, and subterfuges, she claimed. Every official letter I received transformed me at once into a charlatan, and unable to believe in my true feelings, I hid behind pretended sensitivities. I did try, over and over, to tear through my web of lies—when I myself lost my way in them, that is—but I seemed to think this could be done only with one big, decisive lie... And perhaps, she said, and this was the final straw, that decisive lie is all that stuff you write! — You've been leading a double life for ages! she cried. And she could never forgive herself for feeling attracted, at first, by this of all things... by your dark existence! It was a mistake, she said, weeping... and her weeping, for me, had unimpeachable authority... it was a mistake, all attempts to shed light on your darkness are doomed to failure!

I hadn't asked what she meant by *that stuff you write*: did she mean only my secret correspondence, or everything I wrote, that is, my literary work as well? — If it was the latter, this gave me an argument for a counterstrike when the time was ripe.

When my mother got up, between seven and eight, it was time for me to go to bed; first Mother invited me to drink a cup of coffee with her, which I did; I knew I'd have trouble falling asleep anyway. Furtively I swallowed half a sleeping pill... this too was a habit I kept hidden to avoid reproaches... here the two women were in agreement: Mother thought all these chemicals wouldn't really help, I'd do better to live healthy and not overtax my nerves; in my wife's view I had to sedate my guilty conscience before I could relax in bed. — And in fact my wife was right to accuse me of a guilty conscience, for I took the pills from one of her bottles, secretly, every time she was prescribed a new ration by a doctor she was friends with . . . I regularly stole two or three when the bottle was still too full for her to notice; I stole them, as it were, for the long term, stocking up a supply I needed when my reading tours got too grueling. My wife took sleeping pills for granted; she needed them for the phobias that often gave her writer's block . . . as I never had writer's block, in my wife's view I had no need for sleeping pills.

The dose was too small, I realized soon after lying down; I snuck back into the bathroom to take the other half of the pill. Then, as I lay in bed, a sort of sleepless twilight descended on my brain, a haze of exhaustion and unrest behind which the film of my thoughts went on restlessly unspooling. My ears were defenseless against the onslaught of traffic noise from the street; even on Saturday mornings it was twice as loud as it had been on weekdays before the changing of the system, back when the town's industrial plants were still operating. For the first time in years and years I thought of going out again to buy alcohol, but I lay where I was, immobilized, beads of sweat on my brow, unable even to fetch another half sleeping pill from the bathroom. At some point I sat on the edge of the bed, smoking; my mother had already left the flat to run some errands . . . What was he after, the guy who'd ambushed me by the mailbox early that morning?

Could he want money for the letters and cards to Marie he'd pocketed, could he want to sell them to me? Hard to believe . . . All he sought, it seemed, was the gratification of a crude, voyeuristic urge; he wanted to carry on what he'd begun ten years before in the back room of some bleak, poorly lit post office. But how did he plan to continue . . . with my consent, evidently? Had he discovered in my letters to Marie that character trait that so resembled his . . . didn't the word *see*, which he used so obtrusively, actually come from me, from a letter of mine, or even several of these letters? Hadn't my letters, too, displayed a certain voyeurism?

I fetched the half sleeping pill from the bathroom and flung myself down on the bed again: a memory surfaced in the haze of my consciousness, though I couldn't say whether it was the memory of an actual scene, or merely the memory of a fantasy of that scene, the memory of a haze of words in my imagination that I then described in a letter, probably a longer letter to Marie . . . she hadn't answered it, as often happened she said not a word about it; and I remembered that in her silence I'd been seized by a lasting sense of shame, the suspicion that that letter had simply been too lascivious, too tasteless. Now it occurred to me that the letter might not have been tasteless at all, at least not in Marie's eyes. And I thought of the ironic smile with which, often enough, she had requited my failure to act . . .

It was a luminous letter, by no means shadowed by the darkness in which I was so often said to deal. — Marie had once called me a *verbal eroticist*, evidently, so I threatened to ravish her . . . and I described the incident to her so vividly that I'd come to doubt it was just a figment of my imagination. — One day, I claimed, I'd gone to her without announcing myself . . . I believe that in the letter I even asked if she too could recall that sunlit afternoon . . . I never asked her in an actual conversation, which is why I doubt that afternoon's reality . . . she opened the door, and after barely exchanging three sentences with her, I went into the next room, the bedroom, and said, without any transition, that she should undress and lie down on the bed . . . completely naked, I said. She did so, unquestioning, still dazed by the unexpected onslaught, which I carried out in an odd, commanding tone. I stripped as well, down to my undershorts, and knelt on the floor at the foot of her bed. I don't know whether I told her to part her legs; after a time, at any rate, she spread her thighs and bent her knees: her sex was delivered up defenseless to the sunlight that flooded the broad window through the gaps of the yew hedge and over its straight-cropped edge, iridescing in the weave of the curtains. I said not a word, entranced by the sight of what faced me, female, alien, mocking all appellations: no, I had no idea whether I was entranced or ensnared, or possibly dismissed . . . I could reach out and plunge in, but some mysterious mental malfunction prevented me; I was hypnotized by the expression of a mouth drawn slightly crooked, filled with covert irony, offering itself to me and yet in some unfathomable way refusing itself. Marie, too, said nothing, not moving, except that her legs barely perceptibly slid further and further apart; after a long time she asked what I wanted . . . What are you doing down there, she said softly, out in the cold . . .

I could think of no reply, still staring at the curving cleft, which extended down a hand's breath from a little mound until it closed to a seam at whose end, hidden between swells, another opening appeared. My searching eyes returned to the slit that was like a sleeping mouth; its lips were closed, adhering as in breathless dryness. Only in time, in a patch of light, it seemed, that struck them from the window, did the lips grow suppler, an invisible melting that came from within, and parted by a few millimeters. Then the light illuminating

Marie's body from the window grew cooler; barely visible, merely imaginable tremors skimmed her skin. All that remained was one bright reflection, the tip of an arrow of light that pierced the hedge and clung to her body, fragile still, nothingness made visible, and as she moved a bit, growing restless, it darted across her lightning-quick and grazed her sex, now open, beginning to gleam in naked hues. — When this light is gone, then I'll go, I thought...

The image lingered before me when I woke in the evening: it was growing dark; the streetlamp across from the bedroom window had gone on; it was past mid-September, the days growing noticeably shorter; for a few moments I didn't know where I was, then I heard the television, volume muted, in my mother's living room. I went into the kitchen, took from my bag a postcard with a picture by Egon Schiele showing a woman with legs spread wide, put it in an envelope and addressed it to Marie in Leipzig; I didn't write a word on the postcard. — In the morning between four and five, I brought the card to the mailbox; all night I had clicked my way through the countless television programs and kept falling asleep in my armchair... not an image on the screen had the least thing to do with the truth or the reality of life. My mother, who kept nodding off in front of the TV as well, had soon gone to bed... we were two sleepers from a past time; time's tide had caught up with us and overtaken us; the hours of sleep were the only time we still struggled to hold...

Should I give you a light? I asked when, as though out of thin air, he appeared before me in the darkness by the mailbox.

No...he gave his soft, strained laugh, immediately stifled by a coughing fit, no, today I've got my own lighter. But you're right, let's have a smoke before we take our little stroll. — With the cigarette ready in the corner of his mouth, he let the lighter burn longer than necessary; he was still unshaven, we were both unshaven. — Did you recognize me? he asked. And then: Come on, he said, let's walk a ways. That same old way...

I don't have much time, I returned, not stirring from the spot. Actually, I don't have any time at all...did you bring the letters?

I thought you'd be in a hurry, you want to catch the early bus to Leipzig, right?

How could you know that...?

I figured it. You know, we've got plenty of time to think now, we've got much too much time, we don't even know what to do with our time. We spend the whole time thinking, and for me it makes sense that you'd go to Leipzig to visit our little lady friend. But you've got more than two hours left.

I'll spend my time as I please! And where are my letters?

I'll tell you...

You'll *tell* me? Are you trying to say you haven't brought them with you?

It would be pretty awkward for me if you were in Leipzig today and plunked the whole bundle down on the table... and if you told who you'd gotten the stuff from. Besides, this has its risks for me. Where I'm living now, you've got your hiding places, everyone has a hiding place for sensitive things. And you can't put things in or get them out at any time, in front of everyone.

I don't care about that, I just want my letters back. Now we're going to go to where you live, and you're going to give them to me. I'll wait until you've gotten them out. What your colleagues think doesn't interest me. Or what your superiors think... go get them out, and we can both close the file on this one. Or do you want to make a deal with the letters?

A deal? Not at all, don't give me any dumb ideas. I've got the letters in a safe place; I liked your letters, and I still like them. Besides, if we go there now it could end badly for me.

It's time something ended badly for you!

Oh, you're taking a hard line with me... and you think you've got a perfect right to. When I always went easy on you back then, in the old days. — He laughed as he lit his next cigarette; again and again he seemed about to fall into a stroll, his stroll around the block, once even reaching for my arm; I followed him just a short way down the side street, to the big gateway of the former bakery; there I tore myself away and stopped in my tracks.

You know, he said, you can hardly call it living, the place we've organized. It's just holing up. Everyone comes and goes as he pleases... or as he's forced to. Someone'll arrive, and then he disappears again, sometimes for weeks, before suddenly showing up again, and no one asks questions about anyone. It's all pretty crazy, it's chaos... it's probably just that we don't have a homeland now. Today I've still got a bed there, tomorrow I may not, or I'll have a different bed. It's a madhouse, not very cozy, if you know what I mean. No one knows anyone else, and no one wants to know, all kinds of hoodlums could be holing up there. Romanians, Russians, all that scum, let me tell you. And soon the Cubans will come too... they'll come and go and run off with everything. How can you hide anything properly there?

You could carry it on you, on your person.

Oh, they'd even steal out of your ass in your sleep. And you sleep like a dead man there, I can tell you, because the only way to sleep in that commotion is with liquor and sleeping pills.

Then you've finally achieved your true lifestyle, life in the underground, I retorted. That's what you always wanted! And you really think no one would be surprised if someone suddenly failed to show up?

They'd even thank you for it, in absentia, so to speak. There are always too many people there, way too many people, it's a truly artistic existence. Totally Bohemian... as if we'd learned from you people.

He'd talked himself into a frenzy; his voice, barely skirting dialect now, vibrated with a strange enthusiasm. I had to interrupt him:

Let's get back to my letters already...

The letters... well, it's a special situation. Can't you see that they were a kind of identification for me, the proof that I'd belonged? As long as I had the letters in my hiding place, I enjoyed a kind of protection in the house. They wouldn't put me out on the street.

So there are more people who know about the letters?

Not what's in them... I hope. Only the official stamps were important, and the signature mattered. There were some people who'd stopped believing my alias.

Does that mean you don't have the letters anymore? I

took a step toward him; he leaned against the wooden gate of the bakery, rubbing his back against the slats and seeming to bend at the knees, while pulling his dark sweatpants up over his stomach:

I don't have them anymore . . . but I know where they are. I can easily get ahold of them again, with us nothing gets lost, not even now . . . I'll get ahold of them again, you can count on that. How much longer will you be here? . . . I can tell you more tomorrow morning, same place. I can even find out more today, in Leipzig, I could come with you to Leipzig, and while you're with your Marie, I'll get the letters. Tell me Marie's new address, I could come by, and I'd have some positive news for you.

So the letters are in Leipzig now? And you want to come along with me to Leipzig?

In Leipzig . . . they're not there yet, I'm sure of that. But I can meet certain people there!

This is getting to be too much, I said. And you really think I wouldn't mind your showing up at Marie's apartment?

Oh, he said, that's what I always wanted . . . not just to see the little cloud from below, not just to watch her fade away. You'd really do that, go to Leipzig with me? — All at once he seemed agitated; smoking nervously, he laid his free hand on my shoulder as though to clasp me in his arms:

And you'd pay for my bus ticket to Leipzig? The trip has gotten insanely expensive, it's not an easy thing for me . . . I'll have the letters in two days, you can count on it!

You're quite the poor bastard now, eh? I said.

Now, he said, now I am! You're right about that, but such is life. — He dropped his cigarette and wriggled adroitly out of his tight spot, pressed against the bakery gate; as he did, he pivoted, and suddenly I was thrown against the gate's wooden slats. He thrust his face close to mine; I felt his stubble on my cheek:

And I'm telling you, I'll make sure the letters reach their addressee, once I know where she is.

You'll know, you can count on it, I said; and now I embraced him as well. I pulled him to my chest and reached for the knife tucked away behind my back, beneath my jacket and under my belt. With both fists I drove the blade home beneath the left shoulder blade. It was a long, narrow bread knife, and slipped almost without resistance through the jogging suit into his body; he lifted his head and gazed at me in astonishment. It was like something in a movie; when he opened his mouth, bloody foam welled over his lips instead of a sound. I kept holding him in my embrace, kept him from collapsing. Through the little side gate I led him into the bakery yard and opened the door to the former administrative entrance I knew from my childhood. The door stuck, and I had to push it with my knee. He followed me willingly, with tiny, shuffling steps; I set him down on the dusty wooden stairs in the narrow vestibule. He was still gazing at me wide-eyed; I waited until his head fell against the wall beside the stairs. I dragged the grating door shut behind me, picked up the glowing cigarette butts from the pavement outside, and went home. On my way I tossed the butts through a storm drain into the sewer. I made a short detour along a brook, and dropped the knife into the milky, murky water. I saw not a soul the whole way, it was Saturday or Sunday, suddenly I couldn't have said which; the jobless were sleeping away the morning, but it was only just growing light.

Mother was delighted when I told her I'd stay a day longer. I pleaded a headache as my excuse ... I'm not feeling so great, I said, it must be the weather. — Yes, what kind of weather is this, so hot and humid, she said. We aren't getting a proper autumn. But tonight it'll rain for sure, I can feel it in every joint. — I'll fetch you some coal from the cellar just in case, I said.

Mother's rheumatism had not deceived her; when I got up—with the help of two sleeping pills, I'd slept like a stone—it was windy and rainy; well past midnight, when the old woman had long since gone to bed, the showers seemed to let up. As I left the house at last, the pavement gleamed in the light of the few streetlights as though it had been washed. — It was quite easy to find a suitable conveyance in the bakery's spacious yard; I didn't even need the flashlight, with the moonlight that broke now and then through the tattered clouds. Several so-called sack trucks—used in the old days to transport flour sacks—were lying or standing in a corner. I picked out the best one: it would have to move almost silently; the rubber tires of the two small wheels still had to be well inflated. Outside the administrative entrance I laid the sack truck flat on the ground and arranged his body on it, upside-down, his head on the bottom steel ledge; I bent his knees over the truck's upper crossbar, lodging his feet under the two steel struts that formed an X extending to the lower crossbar, then I stuffed his hands under the waistband of his jogging pants, which seemed tight enough.

In his pants pockets I found an ID—not bothering to read the name in the darkness, with the moon behind the clouds once more—a pack of cigarettes, a lighter, and a key ring with two safety keys; I stuffed the things back into the pants pockets, which could be zipped shut. Finally, I covered his face—his eyes, I saw in the beam of the flashlight, were still open wide, but the pupils were now sightless—and part of his torso with several tattered pieces of plastic sheeting the wind had blown across the yard. Instead of carting him down the main street, I took a detour, which cost me a good quarter of an hour, but here, years after the changing of the system, there were still no streetlights to speak of. I reached the wall that separated a sprawling factory complex from the streets at the edge of town: I knew all the tricks for getting through sections of fence that slid open and shut, back doors in the depths of the factory halls that no one ever locked because no one knew about them, through junk rooms, through never-used showers, through twisting passageways in a wing that had last been used before the war, until I reached the old boiler house where I had once worked as a stoker. We used to smuggle alcohol onto the premises through this labyrinth; I was probably the only person in town who still knew the secret route. It wasn't easy to steer the sack truck down the winding passages, across thresholds, over rubble heaps, upstairs and downstairs all the way to the boiler room, as the load seemed heavier and heavier; it was especially difficult, with the flashlight between my teeth, to climb the narrow iron stairs to the top deck of the three boilers, where the coal chutes were. Having reached the top, I had good reason to take a breather; I smoked a cigarette and looked around in the light of the flashlight: except that everything was rotted, rusted, begrimed, and hung with cobwebs, that the table and chairs lay broken in the dust at the foot of the boilers, nothing here had changed... As I opened the chute of the middle boiler—I had to force it—I saw that the fire grates and the ash channels hadn't been cleaned. — How could I describe the strange feeling that seized me at this moment? — Here I'd put in part of my so-called youth; here, somehow, I'd been at home. Indeed, it was a *sense of home* that came to me here, for in this place—and nowhere else, it seemed—I had once been needed...

I tossed his body into the feed chute of the middle boiler; due to the fuel chamber's sharply tapering inner walls, he got stuck just over the fire grate, and using a poker that lay nearby I moved him to a horizontal position; I could no longer see his face, which had slid through the crack of the internal walls, his brow bedded in the ancient cinders. Then I dragged the coal hopper over the chute; the hopper, shaped like the stump of an upside-down pyramid, hung from a slide rail mounted on the ceiling, and could be moved back and forth over the three boilers by means of a chain hoist; the strength this took told me that the hopper was still filled with coal. I wrenched open the hopper's slide gate; rumbling and hissing, spreading a tremendous cloud of dust, the moldered, dried-out, raw lignite, that once-valuable, now utterly deteriorated substance, poured into the boiler and filled it more than halfway full... the corpse could no longer be seen. All the things he had known about me—while all I knew of him was that we had been very similar—had suddenly vanished; I closed the openings of the coal hopper and the boiler chute, tossed the sack truck behind the boiler, where a tangle of steam and water pipes rusted, and crept back out through the labyrinth of passages and courtyards.

Outside it was pouring rain; all at once, autumn had come. I hung my clothes in the bathroom to drip dry, toweled my hair, and drank a cup of coffee in the kitchen. I was in bed even before Mother got up, and slept more deeply than I had in ages, as deeply as after an arduous night shift back then . . . and without a single sleeping pill.

When I arrived a day late in Rhineland-Palatinate, my wife asked whether I'd managed to see Marie. — I wanted to, I said, but . . . The question, her first words, had taken me by surprise, and immediately I'd floundered. — My wife said: I'm surprised to hear that; a young woman called, a painter. She asked me to tell you that Marie died the night of your visit. — Yes . . . I said, yes, I thought as much. — I lit a cigarette and coughed; when my wife finally went upstairs to her room, I was still sitting at the table, smoking. In one flash, or so it seemed, I'd seen Marie before me again: the ironic smile in her eyes was no longer meant for me, it had frozen fast.